"This won't work. You know it won't."

Felicity continued. "If the baby is your priority, then you and I can't..."

"Can't what?" Wynn smiled mockingly.

"You're taunting me, but I don't know why."

"You don't want to *enjoy* each other while you're here?"

"We had our chance. We didn't make it work. And I'm not one for fooling around just for a few orgasms."

"The old Fliss never said things like that."

"The old *Felicity* was an eighteen-year-old kid."

"You always seemed mature for your age. You had a vision for your future and you made it happen. I'm proud of you."

She gaped at him. "Thank you."

"I'm sorry," he said gruffly. "I shouldn't have kissed you. Let's pretend it never happened. A fresh start, Fliss. Please?"

"Of course. We're both here to honor Shandy and care for her daughter. I don't think we should do anything to mess that up."

"Agreed."

* * *

Dear Reader,

My husband and I are lucky enough to live in sight of the beautiful Great Smoky Mountains. From my office window, I can look out on a February day and see the sun glinting off snow on the highest peaks. In April, one of our favorite hikes is awash in delicate wildflowers. During summertime, splashing in cold mountain streams is a childhood pleasure. Every autumn, people travel from all over the country to see fall foliage and catch glimpses of black bears. The Great Smoky Mountains put their mark on those who live here or come to visit year after year.

I love my hero, Wynn. He was so determined from the very beginning not to be defined by the challenges of his early life. He has made it all the way to the top, and yet he can never fully turn his back on his mountain home.

I hope you enjoy Wynn and Felicity's story. It was a joy to write. Have a cup of cocoa, grab an afghan and dig in...

Fondly,

Janice Maynard

JANICE MAYNARD

THE COMEBACK HEIR

HARLEQUIN®
DESIRE™

PLEASE RECYCLE · THIS PRODUCT IS RECYCLABLE

Recycling programs
for this product may
not exist in your area.

ISBN-13: 978-1-335-58141-9

The Comeback Heir

Copyright © 2022 by Janice Maynard

For questions and comments about the quality of this book, please contact us at CustomerService@Harlequin.com.

Harlequin Enterprises ULC
22 Adelaide St. West, 41st Floor
Toronto, Ontario M5H 4E3, Canada
www.Harlequin.com

Printed in U.S.A.

USA TODAY bestselling author **Janice Maynard** is a fan of happy endings! When she left her career as an elementary teacher, she dove headlong into creating and writing sexy, character-driven, contemporary romance. She has published over seventy books, almost fifty of those for Harlequin—a lifelong dream. Janice and her husband live in the shadow of the Great Smoky Mountains. They love to hike and travel. Visit her at www.JaniceMaynard.com.

Books by Janice Maynard

Harlequin Desire

The Comeback Heir

The Men of Stone River

After Hours Seduction
Upstairs Downstairs Temptation
Secrets of a Playboy

Texas Cattleman's Club

Staking a Claim

Visit her Author Profile page at Harlequin.com, or janicemaynard.com, for more titles.

You can also find Janice Maynard on Facebook, along with other Harlequin Desire authors, at Facebook.com/harlequindesireauthors!

For Dolly Parton,
who grew up in rural poverty
and yet pursued her dreams.
Thank you, Dolly,
for your generosity and your respect
for the mountains you call home.

One

November burials were the worst. The day was raw and gray with spritzes of bitterly cold rain. In the distance, low clouds shrouded the foothills of the Great Smoky Mountains. Felicity Vance huddled into her hooded coat and wished she had worn pants. She was keeping her distance from the other mourners.

Her long-sleeve black crepe dress was suitable for the occasion. But she was frozen to the bone. She should have gone for comfort. Earlier, when she arrived at the funeral home and discovered there was no actual service there—only brief words to be offered at the cemetery—she hadn't worked up the courage to go through the receiving line. She had peeked into the crowded parlor that smelled of carnations and grief, and then made a beeline for her car in the parking lot.

Now here she was, wishing she had read the notice about arrangements more carefully.

Witnessing the casket, even from a distance, was a kick to the chest.

Harder still was seeing the chief mourner, the deceased's brother. Wynn Oliver. The man who had once been her whole world.

She watched him now, though all she could see from behind was his broad shoulders elegantly clad in a hand-tailored black wool overcoat. He was bareheaded, the dark, wavy hair seemingly impervious to the heavy mist. The man didn't even have a scarf tossed around his neck.

Her heart ached for him. Despite a wretched childhood—or perhaps because of it—he and his sister had always been close. Shandy was only twenty-nine years old…far too young to die. An aggressive cancer had taken her, leaving only her grieving brother to take charge of her ten-month-old baby.

Wynn and Felicity were four years older. Once upon a time, Felicity thought Shandy would become her sister-in-law.

Life had intervened.

While the minister's voice rolled out over the small crowd, reading verses of comfort from the Psalms, Felicity shivered and curled her fingers inside her gloves. Perhaps she shouldn't have come.

She had seen the funeral announcement in a social media post. Fifteen years ago, Felicity left this small community called Falcon's Notch. Though she now lived in Knoxville, Tennessee—only fifty minutes away—her current address might as well have been the other side of the moon.

Falcon's Notch was a tight-knit, insular collection of families tucked away in a *holler*. Didn't even have its own post office. Students were bused to schools in the nearest town. The residents here were secluded. Most liked it that way, but not all. Wynn and Felicity had yearned to see the world.

Felicity sometimes felt guilty they had left Shandy behind.

But then again, at eighteen and with her entire world imploding, Felicity had been wrapped up in her own hurt and confusion.

She shoved the past aside and brought her attention back to the sad moment being played out in familiar sequence. The green-awninged tent was meant to provide shelter from the sun or rain for the family of the deceased. Ten white folding chairs, two rows of five, sat drunkenly on the uneven ground.

The chairs were empty.

Only Wynn remained of his birth family. Knowing him as she did, he would have scorned the comfort of the chairs. He stood, strong and resolute, until the diminutive minister spoke the final prayer.

Then in a move that broke Felicity's heart, Wynn knelt and dropped a single pink rose on top of the casket. Afterward, he stood and stepped back while the funeral home employees lowered Shandy to her final resting place.

Felicity's eyes burned with tears. Her throat was tight. This beautiful corner of the mountains concealed so much pain. Rampant poverty. Addiction. That last one was why Shandy had never managed to escape. But she had found redemption in getting clean before her child was born.

And now this...

The modest crowd began to disperse. Some of them had come, no doubt, out of sympathy and concern. Others from meddlesome interest. Many would have wanted a peek at the community's most famous local son.

The self-made millionaire. Or maybe billionaire. The number of zeroes at the end didn't matter. Wynn Oliver had been one of them once. A hometown boy made good. He was like a mythical creature in these parts.

After all his successes, Wynn had built a house at the apex of this valley, high in the mountains near the border of the park. Few had seen it, but the rumors of what it looked like circulated.

Wynn's actual home was in New York City. Felicity wondered why he had felt the need to establish a second house at all.

She had been staring at the ground, shifting from one foot to the other, trying to feel her toes when a low, deep voice said her name.

"Fliss?"

In shock, she lifted her head. Stared into eyes that were the green of summer moss on an elm tree. The breath froze in her lungs.

"Wynn," she croaked.

His brows narrowed. "I saw you at the funeral home."

Was that a note of accusation in his voice? She cleared her throat. "You had dozens of people to speak to... I decided I was one too many." She paused, searching for the right words. "I'm sorry, Wynn. So very sorry. Shandy had her whole life ahead of her. It's desperately unfair."

His smile was bleak, no humor at all. "Life is rarely fair. I thought you would have learned that by now."

The edge of sarcasm told her to flee, but her feet wouldn't move. They were blocks of ice that might never thaw again.

When she shivered hard, Wynn took her elbow. "My God, you're freezing." He glanced at her legs, making her gut twist in a strange rush of feeling. "Shandy wouldn't have wanted you to get hypothermia."

"I should go," she said, feeling the pull of his arrogant sexuality after all these years.

"No." He spoke the single syllable without inflection. "I need to talk to you. We'll go to my house. That black SUV is mine. It's unlocked. Get in, and I'll be there in a moment. I'll bring you back later to get your car."

The staccato words rolled over her, creating a haze of incredulity. "Why would I have any reason to do that?" she asked. Now her own voice was snippy and sarcastic.

Wynn's expression turned icy, his eyes shards of broken sea glass. "You owe me, Fliss. This is important."

Before she could respond, he walked away, stopping to chat to others who had come to pay their respects.

Wynn Oliver couldn't *make* her do anything. All Felicity had to do was get in her car and drive away. A couple of things stopped her. One, she was curious. And two, he was right. She did owe him in a weird sort of way. And she had carried that guilt for fifteen years.

She crossed the hillside toward the narrow, graveled lane where the cars were parked. As he had promised, Wynn's doors were unlocked. Felicity got in and groaned in relief. Though the temperature inside the car wasn't much warmer than out, at least she was sheltered from the wind and the rain. She hated pantyhose, but she had worn them today, despite the fact they offered little protection from the elements.

Wynn's car smelled like him. It made no sense really. The boy Felicity had known certainly hadn't been able to afford expensive aftershave. Even so, the faint masculine scent held traces of olfactory memories that softened Felicity's mood. No matter how badly things had ended, at one time she had been Wynn's adoring lover.

She rubbed her legs, wondering how soon feeling would return. If she had gone straight home, a hot shower and comfy sweats would have blurred the harsh edges of this unpleasant day.

Yet here she was.

Fifteen minutes later, the driver's door opened, and Wynn slid into his seat. He brought with him the aroma of nearby evergreens and rain. When he shot her a sideways glance, Felicity stiffened.

His jaw worked. "Thank you for coming," he said gruffly. "I didn't know you and Shandy were still close."

"I wouldn't describe it as *close*," Felicity said carefully. "We exchanged Christmas cards. And emails occasionally. I got a birth announcement. She did share her diagnosis with me. I saw her once at the hospital. She was so damn brave, and yet I know she worried about the baby."

"That's what I want to talk to you about."

He put the car in gear and pulled out in a flurry of gravel. From the cemetery, Wynn's house wasn't far as the crow flies. But the roads to access it were winding and narrow.

Felicity held on to the door handle as they climbed higher. The lane was rutted from recent heavy rains. They lurched from side to side. Their progress continued. The vehicle was equipped to handle much worse.

After they bounced jarringly into one Grand Canyon–sized pothole, Felicity rubbed the center of her forehead where a headache brewed. "You're rich," she muttered. "Why don't you fix this?"

Wynn jerked the wheel and narrowly missed an even bigger hole. "The road deters unwanted visitors."

"Ah."

At last, they reached an iron gate with a code box. Wynn punched in a handful of numbers, waited for the gate to slide back, then pulled onto a paved driveway.

"Thank goodness," Felicity said. "I think I cracked a tooth back there."

Wynn chuckled, though the sound was rusty. As if he hadn't laughed in a very long time. "You always were a smart-ass."

Felicity winced inwardly. She didn't like talking

about the past. She much preferred concentrating on the here and now.

When Wynn's house came in sight, she smothered a gasp. It was magnificent. Somehow, a parcel of land had been carved out of the forest. The house sat like a regal monarch—slate roof, copper guttering, enormous rough logs probably reclaimed from a site out west from the look of them.

"It's gorgeous, Wynn," she said. And just the thing for an unapologetic recluse. "How on earth do you clean it?"

He shifted the gear into Park. "Why is that always the first place women go?"

"We are what we are," she said dryly.

"I have a housekeeper who comes twice a month. She's the mother of one of our old classmates. Discreet and incredibly efficient."

"Nice for you."

They got out of the car in tandem. Now the wind was stronger and the temps lower. Tiny bits of sleet mixed in with the rain. Wynn took her arm as they rushed up the steps. Though it was odd and weird, she was glad of the support.

Inside, the house was quiet. Wynn went around turning on lights. Felicity rotated in a circle, taking it all in. An unpleasant snippet of envy curled in her stomach. As a flight attendant, she regarded her apartment as little more than a home base in between jobs.

But this...

"Wow, Wynn," she murmured. "Your place is incredible."

The main room was huge, and yet at the same time comfortable. The cozy furniture was oversize, perfect for naps and lounging. Bright rugs added warmth to the space. Overhead, an elaborate elk-horn chandelier cast a golden glow.

A massive fireplace dominated one wall. But it was flanked by windows that revealed the misty forest.

Wynn crouched in front of the hearth. "Thanks," he said. "I like it, though I don't get here as much as I had planned when I built it." He lit a match. The already prepared wood and kindling burst into flame. Soon the blaze fed off the larger logs, and the heat finally reached the love seat where Felicity perched.

She kicked off her damp shoes and curled her legs beneath her, pulling a red wool blanket over her lap. Wynn had removed his coat. Now she could see the way his dark pants stretched over his butt and thighs.

He was a powerful man. In every way.

Her host stood. "You want coffee? Hot chocolate?"

"Hot chocolate would be wonderful."

He nodded, his expression unreadable. "Won't take me long."

When he disappeared, Felicity sighed and nestled deeper into the cushions. She hadn't slept well last night, worrying about whether she should come today. Now, as the warmth from the fire thawed her chilled body, she felt drowsy.

That was a bad idea. She needed to be on her guard.

She and Wynn were not friends. She wasn't sure what they were, but they definitely weren't friends.

Her physical response to him told her to be wary of the situation.

After twenty minutes, he returned carrying a large wooden tray which he set on the wide leather ottoman. His tie had disappeared, and he had unbuttoned a couple of buttons at his throat.

The coffee he fixed for himself was black and probably strong…the way he always liked it. For Felicity, he had prepared a cup of steaming cocoa topped with whipped cream. She took one sip and knew it wasn't from a packet.

"This is delicious," she said. "Thanks."

"Of course." He took a seat on the sofa at right angles to her spot on the love seat. "Are you warmer now?"

"Oh, yes."

She buried her face in her drink, unwilling to look at him in this intimate setting. Her body hummed with pleasure—stupid, imaginary pleasure. Like an amputee who still experiences phantom pain, Felicity felt her bones and muscles—even her very cells—respond to the man who had been her first love…her first lover. Fifteen years. Fifteen long years.

They had shared everything. Their hopes, their dreams, their bodies, their love. But in the end, it hadn't been enough. Heartbreak and loss had torn them apart.

She finished her drink and set her cup on the tray. "Why am I here, Wynn? I've enjoyed seeing your house, but I'd like to get home before dark."

He scowled. "Why such a hurry? Do you have a date tonight?"

Her face heated. Was he taunting her? "My plans have nothing to do with you. If you want to talk to me, talk."

"Okay." He lurched to his feet and paced. Occasionally he stopped and added more small pieces of wood to the fire.

Felicity waited him out. She had no idea what he wanted to say. Finally, he leaned against one of the raw wood support beams and crossed his arms over his chest. "Shandy named me as Ayla's guardian."

"I'd heard that. It's a lot to wrap your head around. Is there no one else?"

Wynn shrugged. "The baby's father has never been in the picture. And as you know, our parents are gone."

Felicity nodded slowly. "I heard," she said. "I'm sorry they were never there for you." Shandy and Wynn's parents had both died of drug overdoses on the same night. As adults, as parents, they had been dysfunctional at best. When Wynn was in elementary school, a neighbor discovered Wynn and Shandy had been left alone for hours at a time. Department of Human Services was called in, and the children were removed from the home.

Wynn's mother and father threw themselves on the mercy of the court with an elaborate tale, begging for their son and daughter to be returned. After two months in foster care, Wynn and Shandy came back.

Things were better for a year or two. Felicity knew that Wynn had learned a valuable lesson. Never again did he or Shandy let anyone know about the times they were left to their own devices.

He grimaced. "Even if they had still been alive, there was no way I would let my mother have my sister's innocent baby."

"I can understand that. Where is Ayla now?"

"My housekeeper has agreed to keep her for a few days. I've had all the funeral arrangements to take care of…and I still need to clean out Shandy's apartment."

"And your business in New York?"

He shrugged. "Fortunately, I have good people working for me and with me. I'm just a phone call away."

Felicity nodded. "I don't know what it's like to have a sibling, but I'm sure this hasn't been easy."

His face grayed, betraying exhaustion and the grief he had kept hidden earlier in the day. "It's such a damn waste," he muttered.

Eventually, he crossed the room, shifted the tray to one side and sat on the edge of the ottoman, his knees almost touching hers. "I need your help, Fliss." His beautiful eyes bored into hers, making it hard to swallow, hard to breathe.

Though she wanted to scoot away, she forced herself to sit still. She wasn't afraid. Not really. But this was *Wynn*. Her heart and her head battled over the correct response.

"I'm off for the next five days," she said. "I can help pack the apartment. It will go faster with two people."

His mouth settled in a grim line. "It's not that."

"I don't understand, Wynn." What was he trying to say?

An odd look crossed his face. "In a weird coincidence, I know your boss. He and I served on an FAA advisory committee together a couple of years ago."

As adults, Felicity and Wynn had both ended up indulging their dreams of flying around the world, but in different careers.

Felicity was completely confused. "Okay…"

"I explained my situation. Never mentioned your name. But asked if—under the circumstances—an employee might be granted an extended leave and later go back with full seniority and benefits."

Her stomach curled. Surely, he wasn't saying… "You're not making sense," she said, her voice flat.

Wynn took her hands in his, a clear invasion of her personal space. "I need you, Fliss."

"You already said that. But for what?" Her pulse accelerated.

"I want you to look after Ayla for nine months to a year. Live with me in New York. Care for her. Then when I'm home at the end of the day, I can bond with her."

Felicity jerked her hands away and steeled her resolve. He was asking the impossible. "That's absurd. New York, of all places, must have at least half a dozen highly reputable nanny agencies. You can offer top dollar for salary. You'll have your pick of applicants."

"No," he said, his tone abrupt. "I don't want a stranger in my home or in Ayla's life."

Two

Felicity's heart thudded at a sickening pace. "*I'm* a stranger, Wynn. That baby has never set eyes on me."

His brows narrowed. "True. But you're *not* a stranger. You knew Shandy. You know me. And you're a child of Falcon's Notch."

"What difference does that make?"

"Values. History. Roots."

She shook her head slowly. "You and I *hated* this place. We couldn't wait to get away from here."

"Maybe we told ourselves that. It's hard to escape the intangible things that make up a childhood. Neither of us had a great upbringing, but the mountains were a steady constant. We loved hiking. Even when day-to-day life was wretched, all we had to do was look up and see the vast expanse of time."

Well, heck. If he was going to get all philosophical on her, she was a goner. That was one thing she had fallen in love with all those years ago. The boy who grew up with nothing but had a wealth of knowledge and imagination and a deep vein of wisdom.

Now here he sat wearing expensive, hand-tailored clothing and carrying himself with all the confident masculinity of a man who knew he had conquered demons.

She searched for the right words to shut this down. Wynn was dangerous to her peace of mind. He couldn't drag her into his orbit. She wouldn't allow it.

"First of all," she said, her voice curt, "you had no right to talk to my boss, even obliquely. Secondly, I like my job, and I'm good at it."

Wynn's gaze narrowed. "And third?"

She swallowed. "I don't know anything about caring for a baby."

"Ayla isn't technically a baby. She's ten months old. And though it broke my heart to see this, my dying sister made up an *effing* binder with all the details about eating and sleeping and doctor visits…" He trailed off. His throat worked. His eyes were visibly damp.

"Oh, Wynn…" It hurt her to see him suffering.

"This is probably my only chance to be a father," he said gruffly. "I don't want to screw it up."

Felicity frowned. "You're thirty-three years old. Surely, you've had relationships with women in New York."

"Women, yes. Relationships, no."

She couldn't stand it any longer. Without touching

him at all, she got to her feet and escaped the little tête-à-tête. "It's impossible," she said, keeping all emotion out of her statement. "You know it is. Maybe this is your way of tormenting me for sport."

He stood and tracked her movements, not allowing more than a few feet of distance between them. "I want to be a good father to Ayla. I need you to make that happen." He paused. "It's the least you can do, Fliss."

Tiny spots danced in front of her eyes. He might as well have punched her in the stomach. "That's not fair," she whispered, barely able to speak past the lump in her throat. "You know I didn't do anything wrong."

In that moment, the pain was shockingly fresh and raw. Fifteen years ago, she'd had a miscarriage. A baby she hadn't even known she was carrying. The trauma and heartache had ended her relationship with Wynn, though not immediately.

Both of them had been too immature to handle the grief. She had been focused on her own loss and hadn't been able to understand Wynn's feelings. He had been furious and hurt with no one to blame.

For half a heartbeat, he even questioned whether she had known about the pregnancy and hadn't told him.

She assured him she had no clue, but she understood his knee-jerk doubt. His parents had been habitual liars. Felicity couldn't count how many times they had broken promises to their children.

To say Wynn had trust issues was an understatement.

After the first week of struggling to cope with the reality of the miscarriage, Wynn had asked her to marry him. Even now, she wasn't sure why. Had he thought a wedding ring would soften the pain of losing what had never been theirs to begin with?

At any other moment in their relationship, she would have been over the moon. She *loved* Wynn. But her body and her heart were still healing. She turned him down.

It was the wrong thing to do. Wynn had become a frozen shell of himself. Felt rejected. Lashed out. He had sworn he would never ask her again.

And then he left town, left Felicity behind, and joined the navy.

So much pain. So much loss.

"Please take me back to my car," she said. Her chest hurt. Her eyes stung. She should never have come to the funeral.

He raked his hands through his hair, for the first time betraying a lack of control. "I can't, Fliss. I'm not letting you leave until you say yes."

Her anger flared. "So you're kidnapping women now? Is that your signature move?"

"Not women. Only you." He inhaled and let out a harried breath. "There's one more thing…"

"Don't bother. Nothing you can say will make me change my mind. This is absurd."

His crooked smile was bleak. "I remember every one of the times you told me how hard it was for you not having a mother. When you started your period. When you needed your hair done for a special occasion and there was no money. When you couldn't decide if you were going to sleep with me."

She stared at him in stunned disgust. He was willing to play on her every weakness to get what he wanted. "You cold bastard," she said.

"Think about it, Fliss. Your whole life you dreamed about having a mother, because yours had abandoned you, and your father never settled on a replacement. Girls need a mother. Ayla needs a feminine role model, a feminine touch. Won't you give her what you never had? Nine months, Fliss. Twelve at the most. We'll draw up a contract to keep things nice and neat. And it goes without saying that I'll compensate you for lost salary at the airline."

"Damn you."

He knew he had won. She could see it on his face.

His expression softened. "It won't be so bad. New York is a great city. And you'll have time off. I'm not a monster."

"Let's be clear on one point," she said. "If I do this, it's for Shandy and Ayla. I don't owe you a single thing. The past is the past. Whatever you and I had is long gone."

She couldn't read his face. But his shrug spoke volumes. "Understood."

"And I won't help you with Shandy's apartment. If I'm moving, I have things to do myself."

"Yes, ma'am."

"This may not work," she warned. "The baby may not bond with me *or* with you. Then what will you do?"

His shoulders straightened and his jaw tightened. "I never plan for failure. Only for success. That little girl is all I have left."

* * *

Three days later, Felicity found herself boarding a private jet bound for LaGuardia. Her suitcase was already on board. She'd shipped four boxes of clothes and personal items that would be waiting on the other end.

Panic dogged her every step. *What was she doing?*

The only way she could cope was to focus on the baby. Ayla was adorable. She had Shandy's blond hair and Wynn's green eyes. The little girl would be a heartbreaker one day.

Wynn held the child as he ducked his head to enter the cabin. From the moment he drove Felicity back down the mountain to her car, there had been little communication between the two of them. Only a handful of brief texts.

After all, what was there to say? Wynn had won.

Felicity settled into a seat farther back and fastened her seat belt. She refused to let him see she was impressed. She had known for a long time that Wynn was incredibly successful and wildly wealthy. But seeing his lifestyle up close and personal was a lot to absorb.

He had always been ambitious, even when they were teenagers.

His time in the navy had enhanced his skills, and he had gone to college on the military's dime. Once he was a civilian again, he invented a cloud-based black box that relayed all a plane's vital information in real time. The patent changed his life forever.

As she watched, he leaned toward the window and settled Ayla in her infant carrier that was strapped into the seat beside his. The baby was extremely good-natured and adaptable. Felicity hoped the child would like her, but so far that theory had yet to be tested. Wynn was hogging the child.

Once they were airborne, Felicity was no longer able to ignore her biggest fear. Not flying. She'd been doing that professionally for a very long time. Wanting to keep this private when she went on leave, she'd sanitized the truth to her friends and colleagues.

She was helping a friend. That was all they needed to know.

The fear that kept her sleepless for the last three nights was much more personal. She was going to be *living* with Wynn. Sleeping in his house. Probably sharing meals.

The baby would be no chaperone at all. Her presence might occasionally serve as a distraction, but according to Shandy's now-famous binder, Ayla went to bed every night at seven thirty sharp and slept until morning.

What would Felicity do with all those hours?

When she closed her eyes and pretended to doze, all she could see were images of a mostly naked Wynn running into her in the hall.

In the wee hours of the morning, a man and a woman with a past could make all sorts of mistakes.

And then there was the terrifying truth.

Felicity still *wanted* Wynn Oliver. Physically. Her body recognized his and demanded attention. How was she going to conceal her desire, her urgent, not-so-inexplicable visceral need?

She was thirty-three years old. There had been a handful of men in her bed. Nice men. Decent men. But none of them long-term and none who made her feel like Wynn had when he'd made love to her.

The engines roared. Felicity settled back and tried to relax as the plane took off. The flight to New York was less than two hours. Though she remained seated with her belt fastened—and couldn't see over the seats in front of her—she knew the baby must have fallen asleep, because after thirty minutes, she could see Wynn working on his computer.

Her stomach was jumpy and queasy...filled with equal parts dread and excitement. She would miss her friends and coworkers. Still, this challenge—though fraught with pitfalls—had energized her.

As she gazed at the fluffy clouds outside her small window, she remembered one of the last times she had seen Wynn before his sister's funeral. Felicity had been assigned to the first-class cabin on the Atlanta-to-Heathrow route. Wynn had walked onto that plane and stolen every iota of her professional poise.

After the initial meal, when he lowered his seat all the way flat and pulled the comforter over himself, tucking his head on a down pillow, Felicity had asked to swap aisles with her teammate.

It had required a clunky explanation, but Felicity wouldn't have survived the night if she'd had to walk past a sleeping Wynn for six hours. Even from the other side of the plane, she had still been able to see him.

In slumber, he looked vulnerable and approachable.

She knew that was a lie. When she had brought him his dinner tray earlier, he looked right through her as if he had never seen her before.

His reaction hurt. A lot.

When she thought back to that London trip, the memory still ached. She remembered thinking the overnight flight would never end. The following morning when breakfast was served, Felicity watched, pained, as Wynn smiled at the flight attendant who should have been Felicity.

Only once, just before landing, had Wynn glanced Felicity's way. Their gazes met. Something passed between them, and she knew suddenly that he had absolutely been as aware of her as she had been of him.

That was a year and a half ago. She hadn't seen him since…not until the terrible day of Shandy's funeral.

Felicity barely noticed when the plane hit turbulence. Her thoughts were occupied with Wynn and Ayla, much like they had been since that bitterly cold day at the cemetery.

She learned her lesson at the funeral. Today she wore comfortable black knit pants with a royal blue silk shell and a matching black jacket. It was warm in the cabin. Her blazer was folded on the seat beside her. The low-heeled black pumps sat under the seat in front of her while she flexed her feet.

Why hadn't she asked Wynn more questions?

She knew the answer. After that day at his house, she had been desperate to get home and shore up her weakening defenses. No more contact that wasn't strictly necessary.

She leaned out into the aisle and peeked toward the front of the aircraft. The baby must still be sleeping. Wynn was hard at work. She wondered when *he* slept. She had a feeling his phone never left his reach.

All she could see of him was one shoulder and the top of his head. But she remembered her first glimpse that morning. The same black wool overcoat. Underneath, another expensive suit, this one dark navy. He'd even worn a tie, which seemed a tad over-the-top, but what did Felicity know about the current Wynn Oliver? Maybe he wore those elegant silk ties to bed.

Thinking about Wynn and ties and bed in the same breath was not wise. She was already anxious about the upcoming living arrangements.

She knew he lived in an expensive co-op apartment one block off Park Avenue. He'd promised her it was plenty big for the three of them. And that Felicity would have her own space and her own time away from him and the baby. But that was the funny thing about promises. Sometimes they were just words used as bargaining chips.

Landing at LaGuardia and deplaning with a wealthy, well-known New Yorker was a far different proposition than struggling at baggage claim with the hoi polloi who flew coach. A private car and three employees stood ready to load Wynn's entourage and whisk them away with minimum fuss.

Wynn had spent a great deal of his career working with airlines and FAA officials. He knew most of the people at the airport on sight, even the ground crew. Though his success could have made him dismissive of underlings, Wynn was courteous and kind, probably because he remembered his own humble beginnings.

At the car, Felicity was stunned to see Wynn change the baby's diaper and then take the car seat and install it himself. When she said as much, he shot her a wry look. "Ayla is mine now. I won't cut corners when it comes to her safety and well-being."

"Do you trust *me*?" she asked, still not sure of his answer.

He tightened the last strap and backed out of the car. His gaze sharpened. "You wouldn't be here if I didn't."

Unfortunately, they had hit the city at the worst possible time. The trip took forty-five minutes. As each of those minutes passed, Felicity's anxiety multiplied exponentially.

One thing she could say for Wynn was that his employees were unobtrusive, capable, and highly efficient.

Since he wasn't letting the baby out of his sight, there was nothing for Felicity to do but take in the bustle and beauty of the city.

She had visited New York on many occasions. But never like this. As the car took them closer and closer to the addresses of the rarified elite, Felicity felt like an intruder. What would her position be? She wasn't a guest. Technically, she would be working alongside Wynn in caring for his daughter.

The whole situation made her uncomfortable.

By the time they reached the elegant but architecturally subdued building where Wynn lived, Felicity had made herself sick with nerves.

Again, the cadre of employees jumped into action. The trio had been riding in a separate car at the rear. A dignified doorman beneath a maroon awning greeted Wynn and opened doors. Soon they were on an elevator shooting upward to the thirty-fifth floor. The penthouse, as she was to discover.

Wynn gave her a rapid tour while carrying Ayla. "Kitchen, living room," he said. She saw the usual accoutrements. But also, a rooftop garden.

The outdoor area was dull and deserted this time of year, but Felicity could imagine it in spring. The views of the city would be incredible.

"And here's your room," Wynn said a few moments later.

Felicity paused in the doorway, feeling shock and something else. The faint scent of paint hung in the air. Surely, he hadn't *redone* anything. Just for her. That would be ridiculous. But the proof was in the smell.

The walls were painted a delicate shade of celadon. It was the exact color she had once pointed out to Wynn on a sample card in the hardware department of a big-box store. At seventeen, she had been rhapsodizing about her ideal bedroom. She had even described a cream-and-gold damask comforter, much like the one now covering the king-size bed in front of her.

"It's beautiful," she said, her tone neutral.

Was Wynn disappointed at her answer? His tiny frown made her wonder. "The baby's room is between yours and mine. I'll have her with me for tonight." He opened the door and grimaced. "One of your first jobs will be to set up the nursery. I've spoken with the manager at one of the best baby stores in the city. She already has my credit card on file. I told her you'll be calling and/or coming in to make your selections."

"I'm not sure I know what all we'll need," Felicity pointed out.

"The manager will assist. I told her you and I are novices. I'm sure she'll spend plenty of my money."

"Do I have a budget?" Felicity knew the answer, but she wanted to see what he would say.

Once again, Wynn's eyes held a bleak grief that was vast and heartbreaking. "Shandy wouldn't let me help with her medical bills," he said. "In fact, she deliberately hid from me how close to the end she was. I failed my sister, but I won't fail this baby. I'll do whatever it takes to make sure she grows up happy and healthy."

Three

For the first hour in her new situation, Felicity was left alone to unpack and settle in. She had seen enough to know that one of Wynn's employees was unpacking for the big boss. Wynn and Ayla were in the living room getting acquainted.

Occasionally, Felicity heard Wynn's deep voice and the baby's chortles of laughter. Wynn's words came back to her. *I'll do whatever it takes to make sure she grows up happy and healthy.* Did that mean fraternizing with the enemy to protect the child in his keeping?

Did Wynn hate Felicity for what happened in the past? Surely not. Surely, he understood she had been as much of an emotional wreck as he had been in those days. Yet his antipathy remained.

When her things were tucked away in closets and

drawers and her personal toiletries stored in the bathroom, Felicity ventured out into the luxurious apartment. It was huge. Certainly, far more square footage
than any of the homes in Falcon's Notch.

Felicity hovered in the doorway to the living room.
Wynn's back was to her, so she studied him as he
played with Ayla. In some scenarios, a baby would
have the effect of softening a man, making him look
more sensitive, more human, more tender.

Oddly, that was not the case with Wynn. In the
same way that a lion plays with its cub, no one watching would be fooled. Wynn might be protective of the
child in his care, but he was no less dangerous to Felicity.

He had removed his jacket and rolled up his sleeves.
His arms were tanned and muscular. His thick, glossy
black hair was styled in an expensive cut. A wave of
longing washed over her. She had missed him so much
in those early years. She thought she and Wynn would
be making a life together. Instead, Felicity had been
forced to carve her own path in the world.

Considering the constraints of her background,
she'd done well. She had been lucky to have teachers
who worked with her to find good scholarships. Once
enrolled in college, she had cobbled together work
study and traditional hourly jobs.

Graduating with a four-year degree had been one of
the proudest moments of her life. Then on to her next
goal. Becoming a flight attendant. The process hadn't
been easy. Only 1 percent or so of the hundred thousand yearly applicants were accepted into the training

program. It had taken three years for Felicity to get in. After that, the sky was the limit. Literally.

She had done her time working run-of-the-mill domestic flights. But eventually, the opportunity came to take an international assignment. At last, she began fulfilling the dream she and Wynn had talked about for so long.

But it had been lonely at times…

Now she looked at the man who shared her yearning to see the world. He had achieved his dream, as well.

Had it made him happy?

Inhaling a deep breath and letting it out to steady herself, she walked into the room and took a seat opposite man and baby. "It looks like the trip didn't bother her," Felicity said calmly, though she felt anything *but* relaxed.

Wynn shot her a dark-eyed gaze. "Indeed." He tickled the baby's tummy, eliciting a string of happy syllables. Ayla's sunny smile was at direct counterpoint to the tension in the room.

"Is there anything I can do to prepare dinner?" Felicity asked.

"I didn't hire you to be a cook."

"Don't snap at me, Wynn Oliver," she said, her voice heated, but not enough to alarm the baby. "I don't know why you're in such a prickly mood, but this whole setup was your idea."

At last, he smiled faintly. "Sorry, Fliss. I never like being out of my element. You know that."

She cocked her head. "You're at home in your own place. *I'm* the one who should be bitchy. Not you."

Now the smile broadened. "You're calling me bitchy?"

"You know what I mean." She paused and sighed. "There's a lot of pressure, right? I respect you for doing this. It's a huge commitment."

"Would you like to hold her?"

The question caught Felicity by surprise. "Of course." She had barely gotten to touch the child before now.

Wynn handed Ayla over and watched as the baby grabbed a lock of Felicity's shoulder-length blond hair and sucked on it. Wynn seemed moody again, his gaze hooded, his eyes darker than usual.

Felicity felt her heart turn over in her chest. She had always hoped to have a child one day. But not like this. Already, she could imagine the pain ahead. She would fall in love with Ayla, and at whatever point Wynn was finished with his pseudo nanny, Felicity would be out the door, heartbreak complete.

Wynn shoved his hands in his pockets. "I *am* getting hungry," he muttered.

She shot him a glance. "I thought your minions handled your every need."

"Snarky Fliss. Some things never change. They *work* for me. For the most part, during regular business hours. The clock isn't running now. We're on our own. Do you still like Chinese?"

"I do." Falcon's Notch hadn't been big enough to have chain restaurants or takeout. One small diner, and hot dogs of dubious origin on a revolving grill at the local gas station. That was it. Occasionally, when two broke teenagers pooled their money, they went to the closest town of any size and had date night at the Ming Palace.

"I'll go order for us," Wynn said. "Delivery shouldn't take long. Do you want to try mixing her bottle? It isn't hard. The binder is in the kitchen."

"Of course."

Wynn disappeared into his bedroom to phone in the dinner order. Felicity carried the baby into the kitchen and found the carton of clean bottles and nipples. She measured out formula, mixed it carefully, and smiled when Ayla began jumping up and down on Felicity's hip.

"You're hungry, too, aren't you, sweet thing?"

They returned to the living room and settled into a comfortable chair. Tiny babies usually fell asleep after eating, but Ayla was older. Though she ate enthusiastically, her eyes were alert.

Felicity began a mental list: *babyproof the apartment, research baby development online and/or order books.* She had a lot to learn.

When the doorbell rang, Wynn showed up to pay for the food. He carried the bags into the kitchen and began setting everything out on the table.

Felicity let the baby finish the last of her bottle and then joined her host.

"Right on time," he said.

She told herself not to be impressed. Just because he had ordered her favorite orange chicken with brown rice and a side of two pork egg rolls didn't mean anything. The man's brain was razor-sharp. He probably remembered what he ate for breakfast when he was five.

Her stomach growled loudly. "This all smells amazing," she said.

"Dig in." He held out his arms for the baby.

Felicity handed over her charge…reluctantly. Wynn had poured wine to go with their meal. She drank recklessly, trying to bury her rising dread. What if she accidentally let Wynn know she was still attracted to him? That would be horribly embarrassing.

Besides, it was just pheromones and nostalgia making her feel so vulnerable. The men she dated now were much easier. Less aggressively male. Balanced. That was the word.

Wynn seemed oblivious to Felicity's inner battle. He ate with one hand while holding his niece. "How's your dad these days?" he asked.

Felicity was relieved to find a topic that didn't encompass a minefield. "Daddy's good," she said. "He moved down to Florida several years ago to live near my uncle. The two of them have opened a gator park for tourists. It's embarrassing and cheesy, but he's making a living, and he and my uncle are enjoying their climbing years."

"A gator park?" For a moment, Wynn looked stunned. "Good Lord. I knew your dad was a free spirit, and I always liked him, but wow."

Felicity snickered. "I know. My friends think it's hilarious."

"They're not wrong." His genuine smile did something funny to the pit of her stomach.

Felicity cleared her throat. She needed to get back on track. "What's the plan for putting Ayla down tonight since you don't have a baby bed yet?"

Wynn swallowed a bite of food and nuzzled the little girl's head. "A friend of mine loaned me a portable crib. It will do for one evening. I'll keep Ayla in my room because we don't have a monitor yet."

"Can I help in any way?"

He went still for a moment and then looked up, his eyes warm and bright. "Are you offering to share my bed, Fliss? I'm honored."

"Go to hell," she hissed, feeling her face flame.

He covered the baby's ears with both hands. "Language, Fliss. Really. I thought you'd be more maternal than this."

She skewered him with a withering look that was unfortunately about as effective as a toy arrow against a thick-skinned animal.

They finished their meal in silence. Felicity wasn't prepared to offer herself up for his jibes, and who knew what Wynn was thinking?

Once they were done and the cartons tossed in the trash, she knew she had to try again. "Don't we need to talk about the daily schedule?"

Wynn pursed his lips. "I suppose so. Meet me in the living room in ten minutes. I think this little lady needs a dry diaper."

Felicity's immediate instinct was to offer a hand. But she quashed the impulse. Wynn was a grown man. If he started to drown, he could beg for help. That image was gratifying.

Fifteen minutes later, Ayla sat on a quilt on the floor playing with blocks. Wynn and Felicity had taken seats opposite each other.

He folded his arms across his chest. "Well," he said, "what do you want to know?"

Was he deliberately being obtuse? She tamped down her temper. "Babies do well with schedules. I have your sister's binder. But you've indicated that you want to bond with Ayla whenever you're home. Is that going to be a set time? What are you thinking?"

Wynn leaned forward, his elbows resting on his knees. For the first time that evening, his mask fell, and she saw the depth of his sadness and uncertainty. "I'd like to give her breakfast. I'm always up early. Then I'll do my damnedest to be home by five, although honestly, that's a long shot. My hope is to have dinner with her and be the one to put her to bed."

"I see." She shrugged. "That makes sense." And what about *after* the baby's bedtime?"

Perhaps Wynn was more in tune with Felicity's mental state than she realized. He stared at her. "After she's in bed, I'll be out most evenings until late."

"Work stuff?"

"Sometimes. But mostly social."

The verbal slap in the face was delivered with a steady uninflected tone. But he watched her carefully. Was he expecting her to react?

Felicity swallowed the knot of hurt in her throat. "I understand. That's helpful." She paused. "You mentioned time off. I assume that will be weekends?"

For a split second he was taken aback. She saw it in his eyes. Maybe he didn't like Felicity reminding him this was a business arrangement. He cleared his throat. "Ah…yes. Sundays for sure. And Saturdays after lunch."

"Not all day Saturday?" She frowned.

Wynn sat back, his gaze flat. "Sometimes I won't be home until Saturday morning."

Felicity was ready to get up and walk out. He was intentionally being hurtful and petty. Friday night didn't mean a business trip. Wynn wanted her to know he planned occasionally to sleep over at a lady friend's place. Or maybe there were multiple lady friends.

Her hands trembled, but she wrapped her arms around her waist so he wouldn't see. "I can work with that," she said. "So, all day Sunday. Half a day Saturday. And I assume my other half day can be negotiable…and will include a night away from time to time?"

Dark brows shot up. "Where would you go?"

His glare didn't intimidate her. "I've been a flight attendant for over a decade, Wynn. I have several friends in New York. I know the city well."

"I see."

It was clear her answer didn't please him. That was too stinkin' bad. "I think we've ironed out the details. Bring me the contract and I'll sign it."

"Um…" His cheeks reddened.

"What?"

"I don't have a contract ready yet. I didn't think it really mattered to you. Besides, we haven't discussed your salary."

She rolled her eyes. "If you're so chummy with my boss, I'm sure you have a good idea what I make. I trust you to be fair." She exhaled. "I'll spend time this evening making a list of all we'll need for Ayla. Should I email it to you, so you can sign off on it?"

"Not necessary."

"I've never taken a baby in a taxi before. How does that work?"

"You don't need to worry about taxis. There's a Mercedes sedan downstairs in the parking garage for your use—car seat already installed. Martin, at the concierge desk, has the keys whenever you need them. And if you're not comfortable getting around in the city, just call my driver."

"But what if *you* need him?"

Wynn smiled faintly. "Ayla's needs come first. I'm told it will be that way until she finishes college."

"And you're okay with that?"

"Of course, I am," he said. "I've been given a chance to be a father, to keep my dead sister's memory alive. Any small sacrifices I might make in the process are inconsequential."

There it was again. His reference to being a father. As if somehow, Felicity had stood in his way.

That was ridiculous. He could have been a father a dozen times over by now. It wasn't her fault he was childless. Maybe that was one of the costs of being a genius workaholic.

"If you don't need my help with the baby," she said, "I think I'll go to my room now." She rose to her feet, proud of her unemotional tone.

But Wynn wasn't done toying with her. "Running away, Fliss?" He got up and faced her.

Her eyes widened as temper rolled through her chest. "From what? From you? Hardly."

Slowly, as if he was giving her a chance to back

away, he took her wrist and drew her to his chest. In unison, the two of them glanced at Ayla. She was happy…chewing on a plastic toy.

"From this," he muttered. And then he kissed her.

Felicity felt as if the ground had been ripped from beneath her feet. She should have put her hands on his chest and pushed. Told him no. Refused to let their complicated past intrude on their even more complicated present.

She thought about it. Even in the shock of the moment, she thought about it. For long seconds she held herself stiff in his arms. But the temptation was too great, the river of yearning too deep.

After a hitched breath, she kissed him back. His lips were the same, firm and sweet and hot as sin. He held her as if he had no intention of letting her go, his arms wrapped tightly around her, one at her back and another at her waist.

Afterward, Felicity couldn't pinpoint which of them returned to reality first. But it was likely the baby's fussy cry that broke them apart.

Wynn knelt and picked up his niece. When he stood again, his jaw was tight. But he didn't say anything.

It was up to Felicity. "This won't work," she said. "You know it won't. If Ayla is your priority, then you and I can't…" She waved a hand, unable to come up with a word to describe what had just happened.

"Can't what?" His tight smile was mocking.

"I think you're taunting me, but I don't know why."

"You don't want to *enjoy* each other while you're here?"

"We had our chance," she said curtly. "We didn't make it work. And I've never been one for fooling around just to have a few orgasms."

He blinked. "Why do you think it would be only a few?" He pivoted. "The old Fliss never said things like that."

"The old *Felicity* was an eighteen-year-old kid."

"You always seemed mature for your age. I think that's what attracted me to you. Most of the girls were giggly and silly. You had a vision for what your future could be. You made it happen, Fliss. I'm proud of you."

She gaped at him. Why would he say something so sweet when she was trying to hate him?

"Thank you." The words barely came out. Her throat was tight.

"I'm sorry," he said gruffly. "I shouldn't have kissed you. Let's pretend it never happened. A fresh start, Fliss. Please?"

He seemed genuinely contrite. It was her own fault if his very sincere apology sent a wash of disappointment swirling in her stomach. "Of course. It's been a stressful week. We're both here to honor Shandy and to care for her daughter. I don't think we should do anything to mess that up."

"Agreed."

"Good night, Wynn."

As she turned on her heel and walked out of the room, she felt his green-eyed gaze on her back every step of the way.

Four

After years of waking up in a different city three or four nights out of every week, Felicity had learned to sleep anywhere. A hot shower, a cold room and usually some melatonin did the trick.

She did sleep at Wynn's home, but her dreams were disturbing and at times explicit. When her alarm went off at seven, she rolled over in bed and silenced it, groaning. It occurred to her that she had never asked Wynn what time he needed to be at work.

She threw on a pair of teal, soft knit sweats that complemented her blue eyes and her figure. In fact, when she looked at her butt in the mirror, she raised an eyebrow. *Not bad, Fliss.*

It had been years since she heard that nickname. But now Wynn had her saying it as if no time at all had passed. She muttered beneath her breath as she brushed her hair and swiped on some lip gloss. She was Felicity Vance, a professional successful woman. She was doing Wynn a favor.

Maybe if she kept the power balanced, they would muddle along without bumping heads.

She convinced herself that was how it had to be... right up until she walked into the kitchen. Wynn looked like hell. To be honest, that wasn't accurate. Even rumpled and with dark smudges beneath his beautiful eyes, he was gorgeous and sexy.

The man was wearing a ratty T-shirt and even older jeans. She hadn't seen him like this since they parted ways as teenagers. The casual clothing jerked Felicity into a past she wasn't ready or willing to confront.

"You look like crap," she said bluntly. "What happened?"

He yawned and took a long slug of coffee. The baby was perched on his hip. "Ayla didn't like the portable crib. She woke up every hour or two. It was a long night."

"I'm so sorry. Maybe the whole situation is catching up with her. The poor thing has dealt with a lot of changes recently."

"Yeah. I get that."

Felicity poured her own coffee. "I worked on a list before I went to sleep last night. When she goes down for her morning nap, I'll call the baby store. Maybe I can talk them into delivering the crib this afternoon."

Wynn's smile was wry. "I think you can count on

it. I'm going to be one of their best customers, and they know it."

She leaned a hip against the counter while she waited for her drink to cool. "Do you like being rich?"

He frowned. "What kind of question is that?"

"Well, you always enjoyed setting goals and achieving them. What motivates you now?"

"It's too early in the morning for philosophical discussions," he grumbled. "If you'll hold the baby, I'll scramble some eggs."

"No need. Believe it or not, Wynn, I eventually learned my way around the kitchen...despite my father's addiction to toaster pastries and prepackaged lunches."

"You're not here to wait on me," he said, his jaw tight.

"Relax. Ayla wasn't the only one who had a rough night. You did, too. Why don't you go back to bed for a couple of hours? This is only your first full day of parenthood. You have to pace yourself."

"Very funny."

She touched his arm. "I'm serious, Wynn. I'm here to help with Ayla. Let me do that."

Dark color shaded his cheeks. "I'd go back to bed in a heartbeat if you'd like to join me."

He was toying with her. Trying to throw her off-balance. But Felicity had already decided how to handle Wynn Oliver. If she could.

She squeezed his arm and released him. "If you won't sleep, I'll feed you. Are you going to the office?"

"I don't want to, but I do have a few things requiring my attention."

"Got it."

Felicity raided the fridge for eggs and bacon. The simple meal was easy enough to prepare. She found homemade bread and sliced it for toast. In thirty minutes, the food was ready.

Wynn looked as if he might be in danger of falling asleep sitting up. Her heart turned over. She didn't want to see him as vulnerable. She didn't want to admire his devotion to his niece. She didn't want to *want* him.

But she did.

And it wasn't conceit to think Wynn felt some of the same emotions. When she looked at him, she didn't see the successful entrepreneur. The eyes that stared back into hers were turbulent with emotion, with need.

That knowledge made it hard for Felicity to regard this situation as nothing more than a temporary favor for a friend.

He refused to give up Ayla while he ate. The little girl smiled at Felicity as if she had enjoyed a full night of sleep.

Felicity grinned at the baby. "You're going to have to give your new daddy a break. He's a very important man. And he's closing in on middle age, so he needs his rest."

Wynn tried to glare, but he ruined it with a grin. "Bite me," he said. But the words held little heat.

They finished the meal in harmony. Ayla was entertained with an endless supply of Cheerios. At last, Felicity stood. "Give her to me and stick the little crib in my room. I don't care what you do. Sleep or go to work or do the *Times* crossword puzzle. But Ayla is mine for the next eight hours."

He handed her the baby. "Bossy much?"

"You would know."

She stopped short, her face flushing. The words tumbled out unbidden. Wynn used to tease her about being bossy in bed. It was a joke. He had taught her everything she knew about sex back then...or maybe they had learned together. "I'm sorry," she said. "That comment was inappropriate."

"Oh, for God's sake, Fliss." He ran both hands through his hair, making him look even more rumpled and yummy. "We've seen each other naked. There's no getting over that. You don't have to tiptoe around our past."

"But I don't have to bring it up either," she snapped. "We may have known each other once, but we don't now. We're different people."

"If you say so."

His sarcasm grated. Felicity clutched the baby. "I'm serious. This is my shift. You've said you trust me. So go..."

Felicity had been right about one thing. She didn't know much about taking care of an infant. But she could learn.

By the time she had given Ayla a bottle, burped her and changed her diaper, it didn't take much to get the baby to sleep on her shoulder. She put her in the travel crib and tiptoed out of the room.

She couldn't go far without a monitor. Maybe Shandy hadn't been able to afford one.

Because she didn't know how long this nap would last, she called the baby store immediately. In her mind, she had pictured a matronly proprietor. But the woman who answered the phone—the one whose number Wynn had given Felicity—sounded very young.

Had Wynn dated this woman? Was that why he knew to call her?

She told herself not to be paranoid.

Quickly, Felicity identified herself and suggested emailing the list. While both women were on the phone, the store manager looked over what Felicity had sent. She had a few suggestions and additions. Then she asked about colors. That stumped Felicity.

"Can you get started on the big stuff?" Felicity asked. "I'll check with Mr. Oliver and call you back shortly."

As if Felicity had conjured him, moments later she found Wynn standing in her bedroom, looking at the sleeping child.

He glanced up, his smile wry. "Oh, sure," he whispered. "*Now* she decides to sleep."

"She's probably exhausted from last night." They stepped out into the hall, and Felicity closed the door gently. "Why are you awake? Or why aren't you dressed for work?"

He shrugged. "I tried to sleep. No luck. So I'll get ready and go in a few minutes. Did you speak to the baby store?"

"I did. We nailed down most of the list, but she asked

about colors. Do you want to go with a pink and white theme, or something less traditional?"

Wynn slumped against the wall, rubbing his forehead as if it ached. Probably did. "Shandy wasn't at all traditional. She always followed her own path. I guess I'd prefer something unisex. Woodland creatures, maybe. *Ayla* means moonlight. Maybe something along those lines?"

"Got it, boss."

"Don't make me spank you."

His naughty smile barely registered on the flirtation meter. The man was toast. The truth was, Wynn used to take daytime catnaps a lot. After every time they had sex in fact. But if that was the only way he could knock himself out now, he was out of luck.

"I have work to do," Felicity said, ignoring his sexy talk. "Ayla and I will see you at dinner." She opened her bedroom door, slipped quietly inside and closed the door in Wynn's face.

Midafternoon, Felicity realized that she was going to be earning every penny Wynn paid her. Taking care of a ten-month-old, almost eleven months now, was crazy-hard work. Ayla was mobile, but not yet walking. Her crawl pace was impressive.

It was all Felicity could do to stay one step ahead of her and keep the room babyproofed.

Just after two thirty, the building concierge called to get approval—which Felicity okayed—to accept the delivery from the baby store. After that, pandemonium reigned for at least an hour. The three twenty-something delivery guys were polite, cheerful and efficient. Wynn had paid a hefty premium to have all the furniture unboxed and set up.

Occasionally, the young men consulted Felicity, but for the most part, they knew exactly what to do. One of them spoke rapid-fire Spanish. Felicity caught the occasional word, but she realized her skills were rusty.

Finally, the nursery was ready, at least the basics. Bed, rocking chair, changing table, baby monitor. One box contained wall decals that matched the bedding. Felicity would have to deal with those tomorrow.

Poor Ayla was fussy from missing her nap. Maybe a quick one wouldn't disrupt bedtime too much. Felicity sat in the rocker and hummed a random tune, rubbing the baby's back. The infant was out immediately.

When Felicity laid her in the new bed, Ayla looked small and defenseless. What a huge responsibility Wynn had undertaken. Nurturing a young life was no easy task.

Fortunately, the monitor was charged and ready to go. Felicity consulted the instruction leaflet until she was certain she knew how everything operated. When she saw Ayla on the tiny screen, she felt confident enough to roam the apartment. Wynn's kitchen was a dream. She had missed lunch, so she found some cheese and crackers, plus an apple.

She knew she couldn't let the nap last more than forty-five minutes. Once she finished her modest lunch, she sat in the chair in her bedroom and answered several emails and texts.

Her father was baffled that she was in New York

with Wynn, but she spun the situation in a positive light so he wouldn't worry. Knoxville neighbors agreed to keep an eye on her apartment.

Felicity filled out an online form for mail forwarding. One of her friends offered to collect the little bit of mail that had already been delivered. This trip to New York had transpired so quickly, it had been hard to manage all the necessary details.

When she finished dealing with the most pressing items, she glanced at her watch and went to get the baby. Fortunately, Ayla was already rousing. She rocked up on her knees and gave Felicity a toothy grin.

"Hey, sweet girl."

Felicity scooped her up and nuzzled her cheek. "Let's get you a dry diaper and a snack."

After that, the remainder of the afternoon flew by.

Felicity heard nothing from Wynn. She wasn't too surprised. He probably arrived at the office and found himself caught up in meetings or conversations, especially since he was so late getting there to begin with.

Shandy's binder was very clear about the baby's mealtimes and the things she liked to eat. Wynn had communicated with his twice-a-month housekeeper and had her stock the kitchen before Felicity and he and the baby arrived.

So, Felicity had everything she needed. The new high chair was the perfect size. And it was certainly easier to feed a toddler who was constrained rather than bouncing her on a knee and trying to find her mouth.

Felicity gave Ayla two spoons to play with while

she opened baby food and cut a banana into small pieces. With one final glance at the clock, she knew she couldn't wait any longer. Wynn had admitted that getting home by five was a long shot. Now, it was five thirty.

"Well, sweet thing, your daddy is trying. Hopefully, he'll be here before bedtime."

It was almost six when Wynn showed up. His face was lined with fatigue, but when he saw Felicity and Ayla in the kitchen, he smiled. "Day one, and I'm already failing."

Her heart gave a crazy, erratic beat that she absolutely had to get under control.

"Nonsense," she said. "We've just finished dinner. Your daughter is ready to spend time with you."

Felicity washed her hands at the sink and dried them. "I'll leave you two alone."

Wynn frowned. "You're not staying?"

She hesitated, realizing this was shaky ground. "I thought that was what you wanted. I look after her during the day and you bond with her in the evening? I don't want to get in your way."

The parade of expressions that flitted across his face told her he remembered saying exactly that. "Well, don't go," he muttered. "I'd be glad of the company. Ayla is cute, but she doesn't talk back."

Felicity chuckled. "Give her time." She took a seat at the kitchen table and folded her hands in her lap. Then she changed her mind and rested her forearms on the table.

The key was to *look* relaxed.

Wynn sat beside the high chair and kissed the top of the baby's head. "Hey, darlin'. How was your day?" He removed his jacket and loosened his tie.

Ayla blew a bubble and babbled at him. He grinned, looking more like himself. "I know I'm prejudiced, but she really is a cute child, right?"

"The cutest."

"Did the baby stuff arrive?"

"Oh, yes. Your credit card took a huge hit. But everything is ready to go. Ayla even napped in the new bed, didn't you, sweetheart?" Felicity chewed her lip, feeling ridiculously awkward. "Have you eaten?"

"No. Work was a nightmare. Because I spent most of this week back in Tennessee, things got out of hand."

"I thought you had several capable people working under you."

Now he definitely looked guilty. "I might have a small problem with delegating authority."

"Ah." She hid a smile. His confession didn't surprise her. Wynn was the kind of man who gave every problem the full weight of his attention. He was brilliant and driven. To be honest, Felicity worried there would be no room for Ayla in his life. "You want me to order something?"

"That would be great. Pizza?" he asked hopefully.

"Sure." She rummaged in the drawer where he kept the take-out menus and found one for a pizza place that claimed to have deep dish that rivalled Chicago. Had to admire their confidence. When she stepped into the hall to use the phone, she could hear the low timbre of Wynn's voice as he spoke to the baby.

Felicity placed the order, but half of her attention was on the conversation in the kitchen. She had forgotten to ask if Wynn had an account on file, so she gave the pizza guy her own card number.

When she returned, she realized Ayla was starting to get fussy, despite the attention from her uncle, now her father. "Do you want me to get her ready for bed?" she asked. "So you can change clothes and have a glass of wine? The pizza will be forty-five minutes at least."

"Toppings?"

She stared at him. "The usual. I suppose I should have asked."

His eyes seemed to telegraph a message, but Felicity couldn't decipher it at all.

He exhaled. "The usual is fine, Fliss. But I'll handle Ayla. You've been on the clock all day. Maybe you're the one who needs the wine."

When he and the baby walked out of the room, Felicity felt flat. This situation was never going to work, was it? Wouldn't Wynn have been better off with a stranger, a professional? A woman who wouldn't be tempted to confuse the past with the present?

Had he mentioned *being on the clock* to remind Felicity that their relationship wasn't personal?

It was going to be a long nine months...

Five

That second evening in New York set the pattern for the days to come. Because the pizza arrived while Wynn was still dealing with the baby, Felicity chickened out. She took two slices and a glass of wine to her room and didn't emerge until morning.

Fortunately, Wynn and Ayla fell in love with each other right away. He doted on the baby, and she in turn adored him.

If this had been a real family, Felicity might have been jealous. But everything was unfolding exactly the way it was meant to. Wynn and Ayla were bonding.

Felicity made herself scarce whenever Wynn was home. She wanted him to get comfortable with Ayla's routine, and that meant Felicity had to hold back, even if she was the one who spent the most time with the baby.

It wasn't a contest.

For two entire weeks, the setup worked. But then one Friday evening before Thanksgiving, Wynn forced a confrontation.

Felicity was cleaning up after dinner, preparing to escape to her room as usual, when Wynn strode into the kitchen and took the drying cloth out of her hand. "We need to talk," he said. The look on his face sent a shiver down her spine. His expression was intense, and it radiated masculine pique. His green eyes glowed hot. "What in the heck is going on inside your head?"

"I beg your pardon?"

"Don't play dumb with me, Fliss. I've never been treated like a communicable disease in my own home until you moved in."

Her temper flared. "I've done exactly what you asked me to do. To the letter. And Ayla loves you. So what's your freakin' problem?"

His gaze settled on her lips. "You know what my problem is," he said. The words were husky. They rubbed over her emotions like sandpaper against velvet. "It's nothing new, Fliss."

She took a step back. "Don't," she whispered.

"Don't what?"

"Don't make this personal."

"It's never *not* been personal. You wouldn't even serve me on a flight from Atlanta to London. You swapped sides of the plane."

Heat rolled from her throat to her cheeks. "I didn't realize you noticed."

"That's a lie, Fliss. I could feel you looking at me."

She chewed her lip. "Well, maybe I did. It was embarrassing."

He took a step closer. His gaze focused on her breasts briefly before coming back to meet her eyes. "Is that it? Or were we both shocked and...intrigued?"

"Give me a break." She tried to ignore the ache his words created. "There was no intrigue. Just because we both moved away from Falcon's Notch didn't mean it was some great mystery. You left me, and I went on with my life."

He scowled. "I left because you didn't want to marry me."

"Of course I wanted to marry you. Don't be an ass. But I was physically in pain and emotionally upset, and I didn't know what to do. I hurt your feelings and you walked out on us."

"Tell me the truth," he said. "Did you know you were pregnant?"

She frowned. "No. I *didn't know*. I told you that before."

He stared at her without speaking.

"What?" she demanded. "Either you believe me, or you don't. Why would I lie?"

"Your best friend, Jordana, told me you *did* know. But you hadn't said anything to me because you weren't sure I was the father."

Felicity burst out laughing. "You can't be serious. First of all, Jordana wasn't *anybody's* best friend. She was a gossip and a troublemaker all through high school, and she had a terrible crush on you. Secondly, do you honestly think I was having sex with some-body else?"

A muscle in his jaw flexed. "No. Not really. But I was a kid, and you turned me down. What was I sup-posed to think?"

"Listen, Wynn. I forgave you long ago. In fact, I forgave myself. It was a terrible time. If I'm honest, it still hurts to think about it. But we learned from our mistakes, and we've both gone on to have pretty great lives. Even though you lost Shandy, something came out of that tragedy. You have a *daughter*."

"So taking care of her is just a humanitarian ges-ture on your part?" His features were carved in gran-ite, his eyes hooded.

What did he want from her? Certainly not a do-over. It was too late for them. A teenage love affair gone wrong didn't translate into anything meaningful a decade and a half later.

"It's a favor," she said quietly. "One I'm happy to do for you and Ayla in memory of Shandy. You said nine months, and the clock is ticking. I have friends and a career I'll want to get back to sooner than later."

She was in danger of overplaying her hand. But if she showed any chinks in her armor, Wynn might talk her into an affair. It wouldn't be hard. The thought of being intimate with him again made heat rush through her midsection.

Wynn, the teenager, had been intense and sweet and eager to please. Wynn, the sophisticated man, would probably destroy her. She couldn't risk it.

"Fine," he said, the word curt. "Hide out in your room

if that's what you want. But you can't tell me you haven't imagined what it would be like. The two of us. In bed together."

"It's late," she said, her throat tight.

"It's not even nine." He wasn't giving an inch.

She straightened her spine. "Don't push me, Wynn. You won't like what happens."

He raised an eyebrow. "You're threatening me? Wow, Fliss. You've grown into a hell of a woman. I'll give you your space, but don't expect me to ignore you. It won't happen."

Saturday morning Felicity found a note under her door. Wynn's dark scrawl sent a terse message. "I'm here. Take the whole day."

Though it was cowardly, she dressed and sneaked out of the apartment while he was in the baby's room.

After hailing a cab, she sat back and watched the city flash by her window. How was she going to resist him? He would never force her. That wasn't his style, nor was it the problem.

Felicity was the weak link.

She found herself at Rockefeller Center watching crews decorate the enormous Norway spruce that would be lit up in all its glory the Wednesday after Thanksgiving. Even in daytime, the tree was impressive.

Thinking about the holidays made her stomach twist. She rarely celebrated with her father. Instead, she and a group of friends with similar situations often took turns hosting.

Without Shandy, Wynn had no family either. Why

was Felicity only now thinking about the ramifications of Thanksgiving and Christmas? Taking care of Ayla was all-consuming. For a novice, the recent learning curve had been significant.

Only today—seeing the heart of the theater district begin to flaunt the holiday spirit—did Felicity understand what she had done. Unless she could think of an excuse to leave, she was going to be spending a long weekend with Wynn and the baby. The parade and the TV movies. Turkey and pie and all sorts of warm feelings.

That would only lead to more temptation.

Though it was hard, she made herself stay out until dark began to fall and the temperatures dropped. She window-shopped and did a bit of real shopping, but the day felt hollow.

Where she really wanted to be was at home with Wynn.

Because that need and want was so very strong, she forced herself to wander the streets.

At last, cold and tired, she made her way back to the apartment. After rummaging for her key, she opened the front door and let herself in. The first thing she heard was the sound of Wynn's steady voice singing "Wheels on the Bus."

She stopped in the foyer, her legs wobbly and her eyes damp. If she had not miscarried all those years ago, she and Wynn might have a fourteen-year-old son or daughter right now.

It was undoubtedly for the best. Everyone knew the statistics for teenage marriages—particularly ones where the couple *had* to get married—were dismal. While sitting at the dentist office one day, Felicity had seen a magazine article claiming high school sweethearts who got married while still teenagers had only a 54 percent chance of having a marriage that lasted a decade.

Even if she *had* accepted Wynn's impulsive proposal after her miscarriage, there was a very good chance they might have divorced five years ago. Or maybe six or eight.

The subject depressed her.

She found her housemates in the large living room. The thick, lush carpet was strewn with a variety of baby toys. Wynn lay sprawled on his back on the floor. He held Ayla's hands as she sat and bounced up and down on his stomach.

The baby's squeals of glee were contagious.

At last, Wynn noticed her standing in the doorway. "I was about to send out a search party," he said, his tone light. "Did you get lost?"

"No."

His gaze settled on her shopping bags. "Retail therapy?"

"A bit." Why was it that when Wynn dressed casually, her thoughts immediately dived into the past? Tonight, he looked younger, more like the boy she had crushed on when she was sixteen. They had started dating on her seventeenth birthday. By her eighteenth, she knew she was in love with him.

Had it been puppy love? By definition?

She didn't think so. Because she and Wynn had suffered through unorthodox childhoods, they had been mature for their years. They knew what they wanted. It was a short list: to see the world, and to have each other.

Wynn cocked his head, perhaps wondering why she still stood there, packages in arms. "You hungry?"

"Not really." To get out of the wind at lunchtime, she had popped into her favorite Cuban restaurant and ordered a huge meal. She filled her stomach with fabulous food and killed an hour and a half at the same time.

Eventually, she'd had no choice but to go out into the cold.

"There's plenty of leftover sushi in the fridge," he said. "If you want it later."

"Okay. Thanks. If you'll excuse me, I'll go change."

He sat up, shifting Ayla to the floor. "Are you okay, Fliss? Did something happen today?"

She dumped her bags and purse in the nearest chair. "Do you realize this week is Thanksgiving?"

From his expression, it was clear he hadn't put that together. "Oh. I guess with the funeral and moving Ayla here to New York, the calendar got away from me."

"What do you usually do for the holiday?"

He shrugged. "Watch football and drink beer."

Felicity wrinkled her nose. "Don't you think you should make an effort now that you're a father?"

"Ayla won't remember." He set the girl on the rug and stood, stretching.

For a moment, Felicity caught a glimpse of his flat

belly before he lowered his arms, and the shirt came back down. She sighed inwardly. "But *you* will. Traditions are important."

He picked up a purple stacking cup that had rolled out of Ayla's reach and gave it to the little girl. "What are you trying to say? I assumed you would want the long weekend off."

"Well…" She felt her face heat. "Ordinarily, I would be working a chunk of the holiday…biggest travel day of the whole year and all that. But since I'm on hiatus, I'd be happy to help pull a meal together. Only if you want me to," she said hastily.

His eyes warmed as a smile kicked up the corners of his sexy mouth. "That sound great, Fliss. There's a gourmet shop around the corner that sells whole turkeys fully baked. Maybe you and I could wrangle the sides."

"Oh, good," she said, making a face. "The thought of tackling a turkey for the first time scared me."

He chuckled. "Yeah. Me, too. I'm not a fan of food poisoning."

When she went to pick up her bags, he stopped her. "Don't disappear when I put the baby to bed, Fliss. Let's have a glass of wine and kick back. Please."

Her heart raced. She measured her words. "Sure," she said. "That would be nice."

His slow smile warmed her body in places that should be ice-cold. She and Wynn were *not* dating. They were barely even friends. She was doing him a favor out of the goodness of her heart. Or more honestly because she felt she owed him something for the past. They had both been hurt, but she hadn't been able to see his pain for her own. She'd had to juggle more grief when he left.

No matter how hard she tried, she couldn't forget the memory of that hungry, driven adolescent who had made her the center of his world for a brief time.

She escaped, and in her bedroom, spread her purchases on the bed. It was Saturday night. She and Wynn weren't trying to impress each other. It was perfectly acceptable for Felicity to choose comfort over vanity.

At an upscale vintage shop on a side street today, she had bought a pair of soft, stonewashed denim jeans. In some places, the pale blue cloth was almost white. She could almost imagine a teenage girl with a flower in her hair wearing the jeans to Woodstock.

That was before her time. Heck. That was even before her father's time. But she liked the image of several thousand people singing together and feeling the freedom of young love.

On a whim, she found an old Rolling Stones T-shirt still tucked away inside her suitcase. She wasn't even sure why she had brought it to New York except it was an item of clothing she associated with comfort.

With the patterns on the front, she could even skip a bra. Just the thing for a Saturday night at home. The pants fit as well as they had in the small dressing room earlier today. She left her hair down and braided one small section to fall beside her cheekbone.

Her blond mane brushed her shoulders, but it had been longer still in high school. Wynn had liked wrapping it around his fist and teasing her. Like she was his harem girl. Or a submissive.

Those games had been few and far between. Felicity was too naive back then to understand the allure of power dynamics. Besides, vanilla sex for two kids who were new to physical intimacy was more than enough excitement.

When she walked into the living room, Wynn had the drapes open, framing the dramatic skyline with its myriad lights. The only other illumination in the room came from a duo of small lamps and the glow of the gas logs in the fireplace.

He smiled at her. "I made you hot chocolate. But you don't have to drink it if you'd rather have wine."

"Maybe I'll have both," she said, feeling reckless.

He raised his eyebrows but didn't say anything.

Felicity chose the love seat. It was small enough that Wynn wouldn't try to sit beside her. The sofa, on the other hand, might have been dangerous. In the end, Wynn sat there on his own, leaning back, his sock-clad feet propped on the coffee table.

The ambiance was intimate. Comfortable, but with an edge of awareness that made her nerves hum. "So tell me about the adoption," she said. "I'm assuming it's straightforward?"

"My lawyer seems to think so, especially with the will naming me as guardian. Ayla's birth certificate doesn't list a father. I think Shandy knew who he was, but she kept her secret to the end. So I can't imagine this guy showing up out of the blue. Surely Shandy would have told him...even if he was a lowlife."

"Your sister dated lowlifes?"

"She got into trouble with drugs. You know that. So yes…there were several questionable guys in and out of her life over the years. But once she found out she was pregnant, she quit cold turkey. Everything. Booze. Pills. Everything. My sister had determination."

"I liked her, Wynn. Even when we were all kids. I'm sorry she had such a hard life."

"Yeah." He sighed. "I didn't mean to bring down the mood."

"You didn't. We can't escape the past. Especially not our families. What ever happened to your friend Matthew? Did he get out of Falcon's Notch? I know he helped his dad at the mechanic shop."

Wynn rested his arm on the mantel, his gaze pensive. "Matthew enlisted, too. Ended up in the marines, high-level spy stuff. I haven't heard from him in six or seven years."

In that instant, Felicity saw the loneliness in Wynn Oliver. He had achieved his dreams, but at what cost? Maybe he saw Ayla as his salvation.

"I think I will have that wine," she said. "I'm still thawing out from my day on the town."

He poured a glass of Chablis and brought it to her. Their fingers brushed, his warm, hers cold. "Sit closer to the fire," he said. "You need to get toasty."

Parts of her were plenty hot.

But she moved to a small armchair near the hearth. "Not to beat a dead horse, but what if Ayla's father did show up and tried to claim his parental rights? Wouldn't it hurt your case to be a single father?"

Wynn sat on the hearth and faced her, their knees almost touching. When he tipped back his head to drink his wine, she saw the muscles in his throat ripple.

At last, he set his glass beside him and stared at her. "Are you offering to be my wife, Fliss?"

Six

"Why do you do that?" she muttered. "Do you like embarrassing me?"

"No. Not really. Maybe I just enjoy seeing your beautiful skin turn pink. Like a dogwood blossom in spring."

"Stop it." She had consumed *her* wine too quickly. Now her head spun. "I asked you a serious question, but you don't miss any chance to make me uncomfortable."

His eyes looked less green in the low light. "Believe me, Fliss. I'd like nothing more than to make you *very* comfortable." His fingertip traced a small circle on her knee. "I like these jeans. You look eighteen again."

She put her hand over his, meaning to push him away. But when she felt how hot he was, how alive, she relented. Twining her fingers with his sent her stomach into a free fall. "I'm not that girl anymore. If you're looking for the fountain of youth, you'll have to search elsewhere. I've gained fifteen pounds since those days. I have wrinkles. Maybe even one or two gray hairs."

"Liar," he said with a grin.

"I've been wondering what it would be like to kiss you again," she whispered, rubbing her thumb over the back of his hand. "But I can't ask, because it wouldn't be fair if I'm not going to sleep with you."

"That's a conundrum," he said. His words got all low and croaky. "But I can handle it."

"What if I can't?" It was an entirely honest question. She was bone-deep scared.

"I won't let anything hurt you," he swore.

"Unless you're the one doing the hurting."

He winced. "Do you think so little of me?"

"I think you have your life all mapped out. I do, too. To play games would be dangerous."

"You don't think we could keep it light and easy?"

She lifted her hand and caressed his eyebrow. It was silky and thick. "Knowing us, no. Of course, you might have changed. You may flit from one flower to another these days."

He groaned. "That's the worst metaphor I've ever heard."

"At least you *know* it's a metaphor. Otherwise, you might never have passed senior English."

He bowed his head. His shoulders slumped. Then he looked up at her with so much pain on his face she was shocked. "I'm sorry about the baby, Fliss. You were in agony, and I couldn't do a damn thing to make it better. I've carried that with me for fifteen years."

"You're absolved," she said quietly. "Nothing about what happened was your fault. It happens to dozens of couples every day. Not unusual at all."

"Then why did it feel like our world ended?"

They sat there staring at each other. Slowly, with what seemed like no intent at all, they leaned forward. She felt his breath on her cheek, smelled the wonderful scent of warm man and aftershave.

He cupped her face in his hands. "I like having you under my roof. Tell me this isn't a burden to you. Tell me I haven't ruined your life."

She swallowed, trying to find the air that had escaped her lungs and left her breathless. "My life is just fine."

"Do you still want to kiss me?"

"I said I *wondered* what it would be like. Not the same thing at all."

"Splitting hairs, Fliss. Maybe you should have been a lawyer instead of a flight attendant."

The urge to press her lips to his was fierce. Finally, she realized he wasn't going to take the leap for her. He wasn't going to let her play the victim. This was the man who swore he would never propose to her again. Maybe that proclamation included lesser activities as well.

She lifted her chin. Closed her eyes. Puckered up. Just to see what would happen.

After ten seconds ticked by with no kiss, she lifted

her lashes and looked at him, feeling foolish. His sexy smile made her sweat. "Maybe I don't even like you," she complained.

"That would be a problem," he said solemnly. "For the kissing, I mean."

"Why do *I* have to do it?" she asked.

"Do what?"

"Start something. In the movies, the kiss is magic. And the guy initiates it. I'm almost positive."

He smirked. "You must have signed up for that really cheap cable. The one where they show only old movies. Twenty-first-century women are vixens. Warriors. Princesses. They don't wait for some dumb jock hero to get around to the first kiss."

"But it wouldn't *be* our first kiss," she pointed out. "So why can't you do it?"

"You know why, Fliss. You're living under my roof. Doing me a favor. For me to make the first move would be sleazy."

"I like sleazy," she said desperately. "And I swear I'll respect you in the morning."

He threw back his head and laughed. The sound was deep and magical, luring her to her doom.

Felicity felt the spell wrap its tentacles around her, and she didn't even care. "Oh. All. Right," she said. "Come closer."

He blinked, as if she had surprised him. "I thought we were flirting for the hell of it. Are you sure, baby? Or is it the wine talking? You never could hold your liquor."

"Shut up, Wynn. I'm going to kiss you." Slowly, as

if he was a wild animal who might bite, she wrapped her arms around his neck. "You have the most beautiful eyes. I've never seen that color on any other man."

"Have there been a lot?" He shook his head, visibly chagrinned. "Sorry. I didn't mean to say that."

She rubbed her nose against his, teased his upper lip with the tip of her tongue. "It's okay. We're both adults. I don't mind giving you my number. It's three. Four if you count a blind date where the guy kissed me in the back of an Uber, groped my boobs and threw up in my lap."

"You're making that up."

"Nope."

"Men really are pigs."

Felicity smiled. "Present company excluded."

His chest rose and fell rapidly, despite his apparent calm. "I'll take that as a compliment. But Fliss…"

"Hmm?" She traced the shell of his ear with her fingernail, first the left, then the right.

"Fliss…" This time louder.

"Hmm?" She was in a daze, enjoying the naughty game.

"Are you *ever* going to kiss me?"

She leaned back so she could see his face. The note of desperation in his voice was gratifying. "Is there a problem?" she asked, the words dripping with innocence.

"Don't push me too far, darlin'. I have my limits."

The male frustration in his voice made heat curl between her legs. "You can take over *any*time. I'm not stopping you."

He gripped her shoulders—tight, but not too tight. Letting her know he meant business. "Kiss me, Fliss. Or go to your room."

"Ooh," she said. "Are we playing headmaster and schoolgirl now?"

His face darkened. His brow was damp, perhaps from sitting too close to the fire. "Swear to God, Fliss. This isn't funny. Do it."

She leaned closer and pressed her lips to his, sliding her tongue inside. The taste of him had aged well. Intoxicating but with a hint of sweet.

Somebody gasped.

Felicity was electrified. Feelings she had buried deep burst to the surface in a kaleidoscope of color. It was like seeing her previous life unfold before her eyes. She saw who she had been, what she had lost, and how she had been born again like a phoenix from ashes.

Wynn's embrace should have been familiar. Maybe it was…somewhere down deep. But the man he had become was entirely new. His passion, his confidence. His absolute certainty about what he wanted.

He seized control of the kiss before the five-second mark, his mouth dueling with hers. She was desperate to get closer. How could something hatched so recently feel full-blown, mature, deeply sensual?

She ran her fingers through his thick hair. When she caressed his scalp, he groaned. That sound tapped into something she had tried to forget. With Wynn, years ago, she had felt like the truest version of herself. She had reveled in her femininity.

Now those feelings returned. She felt her body thrum with delight. It was melting and yearning and reaching for something just out of sight. Sex, yes, but more than that. She wanted the all-consuming passion.

A tiny noise intruded upon her pleasure. A familiar sound, but faint. "Wynn," she said softly.

He caught her bottom lip between his teeth and tugged.

Oh, lordy. She arched her back, trying to get closer. Her fingers dug into the soft cotton of his shirt. "Wynn." She said his name again, with a touch of desperation this time.

"What?" he asked, the single word sharp as he cupped her braless breasts through her T-shirt.

"I think the baby is awake."

He froze. Pulled back. Rested his forehead against hers. "Unbelievable. How do young parents *ever* have sex?"

Felicity stood and smoothed her shirt. "First of all, you and I weren't having sex. And secondly, I think young parents do it out of desperation whenever and wherever they can."

The sounds from the baby monitor were louder now. "I'll go get her," he muttered. At the door, he turned around. Pinned her with a sharp green gaze. "Do not sneak away."

"I won't sneak. But I'll tell you to your face. I'm going to my room. Ayla probably saved us from doing something stupid. I'm taking a step back, Wynn. You should, too. You're grieving and your life is over-whelmed with new responsibility. I'm a part of your past. None of those are reasons to start a physical relationship."

He scowled at her. "It must be nice to have all the answers. I guess that comes from smiling and delivering a thousand of those *fasten-your-seatbelt* speeches."

She blinked. "Wow. You're not very nice when you're frustrated."

"Get used to it," he said. And he walked out.

Sunday morning, Felicity picked out a red turtleneck and gray wool pants, pairing them with a thigh-length black wool coat and black ankle boots. Her over-the-shoulder black bag held everything she would need for the day.

Last night after leaving Wynn to deal with the baby, Felicity had sent a group text to five of her coworkers who were based in New York. She suggested brunch at the Plaza, and three of her friends were available.

This time, she didn't try to sneak out of the apartment. She found Ayla and Wynn in his bedroom. "I'm heading out," she said.

Wynn's expression was hard to read. "You look nice. More shopping?"

"No. Brunch with friends."

"Ah."

"I'll probably be gone most of the day. I think we're going to the Met afterward. I haven't been in ages."

"Sounds like fun."

Felicity felt guilty, and she didn't know why. Sunday was her day off. Ayla wasn't *her* daughter.

"Do you need anything before I go?" she asked.

"No, thanks."

She chewed her lip. "Are you angry with me?"

"Why would it matter if I was?"

"Because nine months is a long time for us to co-exist in a hostile environment."

A small grin tipped up the corners of his mouth, erasing his odd mood. "*Hostile* is a strong word."

"We're wrapped up in this weird place between nostalgia and practicality."

"It doesn't have to be weird. You and I are friends. One friend helping another."

"Don't make me out to be a saint. You're replacing my lost salary," Felicity pointed out.

"I know you, Fliss. I suspect you might have done it for nothing if I had asked. Right?"

His question took her by surprise. But she gave it serious thought. "You're right," she said slowly. "I like helping people."

"I'm sorry if I made you uncomfortable last night." His words were strangely formal.

"Don't be dumb," she said, feeling cross and torn in a dozen directions. "I had my tongue down your throat, so I think we can safely assume the feeling was mutual. But that doesn't mean it was smart."

"So many rules," he said. "Don't you ever want to throw open that emergency door midair and see what happens?"

She chuckled. "Now I *know* you're kidding. I thought your daredevil days were behind you."

"I pay a crap ton of taxes. I have a hefty mortgage and health insurance. But I'm still the same guy inside."

Was it true? Was the teenage boy Felicity fell in love with still part of this complex, mature, oh so sexy adult male?

"I need to go," she said, glancing at her watch.

Wynn held up Ayla's hand and used it to wave. "We'll miss you."

Her heart clenched. Spending a lazy Sunday afternoon in the apartment with the two of them sounded wonderfully appealing. But that was exactly why Felicity was going out.

She had to avoid temptation, and she wanted to remind herself that her life and her world were only on hold.

When she arrived at the grand old hotel, Reagan, Paul and Rico hugged her. "I heard you aren't flying right now," Rico said. "What's that all about?"

"I'll tell you the whole story while we eat."

Their table in The Palm Court was lovely, the food and service even better. Felicity enjoyed the meal, but far more wonderful was being with her friends again.

To outsiders, they were an unlikely foursome perhaps. Reagan was Connecticut old money, a black-haired blue-eyed debutante who drank Scotch and cussed like a sailor. Paul had moved to the East Coast from LA years ago. After trying to make it as a musician, he still sang in bars and clubs when he wasn't flying. Rico came from a strong Puerto Rican clan in Queens and was the first of his family to graduate from college.

Despite all their differences, Felicity and the other three had trained together and remained good friends.

She realized that in every way that mattered, these three people were the part of the family she had *chosen* in life.

Paul finished his mimosa and tapped his spoon on his glass. "Enough chitchat. Tell us why you've called this meeting."

Felicity laughed. "Can't a woman just miss her friends?"

Rico shook his head slowly. "You forget how well we know you, *chica*. You wouldn't give up your job for a whim."

Reagan nodded. "You never even take sick days. This must be really big. Unless you're dying." She gasped. "Is that it? Are you dying?"

"I'm *not* dying." Felicity sighed. "It's a long story."

The other three stared at her. Paul patted her hand. "Spill, girl. We've got all the time in the world."

Felicity told them everything. Starting with high school and including Shandy's funeral and then bringing the story full circle to Ayla and Wynn and her new address in New York. She didn't talk about the high school sex or the more recent kisses that had shaken her foundation and made her stomach do crazy flip-flops. But she admitted she was rethinking her decision.

Rico pursed his lips. "I didn't even know you liked babies."

"I don't *not* like them," she said, feeling defensive. "I'm learning on the job. Little Ayla is a sweetheart."

Reagan's jaw dropped as she began to put the pieces together. "Wait a minute. Is this Wynn guy the one on that flight from Atlanta to London?" The one who flustered you so much you made me swap aisles so you wouldn't have to speak to him?"

Three sets of eyes stared at her. Felicity couldn't help the blush that spread from her throat to her cheeks. "Yes," she muttered.

Paul shook his head slowly. "You'd better get out of that apartment ASAP. I think Mr. Genius is looking for a wife to be his baby mama."

"Either that," Rico said, "or our boy Wynn is looking for some action on the side."

Reagan, usually the comic relief in the group, was uncharacteristically serious. "It sounds like he broke your heart once upon a time. I wouldn't let him do it again."

Seven

Felicity had a wonderful day with her friends. The meal at the Plaza. The visit to the Met. So much talking and laughter. They finished off their excursion with dinner at a hole-in-the-wall pizza place.

Yet if she were honest, Wynn was always in the back of her mind. His quick wit. His sexy green eyes and lazy smile. The taste of his firm lips. The feel of his hard, masculine body when he held her close.

She was wading into some very deep water.

Ordinarily, she prided herself on keeping promises and following through on commitments. But what if she had made a big mistake?

By the time she said goodbye to her friends and hailed a cab, she had worked herself into a tizzy. If she was going to quit, she needed to do it now, before she lost her nerve.

Or before she ended up in Wynn's bed.

The baby was asleep when she let herself into the apartment. Wynn was in the living room, sprawled in a chair, doing something on his iPad.

He looked up and gave her a terse smile. "Nice day?"

"Very." She dropped her bag in a chair and shed her coat and shoes. "How were things here?"

He frowned. "I'm not sure. Ayla was fussy. And she ran a fever this evening. I may have to take her to the pediatrician in the morning."

"Oh." Felicity's heart sank. This would be a bad time for her rehearsed speech. "It *could* be teething," she said. "I bought a baby book when I got here. I've been reading a couple of chapters each night. Apparently, it's not uncommon for little ones to be feverish when a new tooth is about to break through the gum. But there are remedies we can try."

Wynn stood and stretched. "You bought a book? And studied it?"

"Yes. Why are you surprised?"

"Not surprised. But it means I chose the exact right person to take care of Ayla."

"Lots of people can look after children," she said, laying the groundwork for her change of heart. "It's not so much a matter of skill as it is common sense and kindness."

"Maybe so, but I'm still damned grateful you were willing to love and protect Shandy's daughter."

Not fair. If Wynn was going to drag the dearly departed into the equation, how was Felicity supposed to walk away?

"I saw the picture you posted on Instagram this afternoon," Wynn said. "Very chummy."

The sudden change in topic caught Felicity off guard, but not as much as finding out that Wynn had an Instagram account. She cocked her head and studied him to see if an alien had inhabited his body.

"You're active on social media?" she asked, trying to make sense of that. It wouldn't compute.

Wynn shrugged. "I wouldn't say *active*, but yes. I have all the usual accounts. It's a necessity for business these days."

"Right…" She wasn't buying it. "What picture are you talking about?"

"The one with two hot guys flanking you, each with an arm around your waist."

Felicity grabbed her phone and pulled up the post in question, trying to look at it from Wynn's perspective.

Reagan was standing in the left of the frame, laughing, a small distance from the other three. Paul and Rico were hamming it up, leaning their heads on Felicity's shoulders and hugging her.

Their waiter at the Plaza had taken the photo.

"You have a problem with the picture?" she asked, feeling her temper simmer.

"I didn't know your pool of male admirers was quite so large…or so *varied*."

"It's two men, Wynn. Longtime friends. I was happy to see them."

"I'll bet you were," he muttered.

She ground her teeth. "I'm giving you twelve hours a day, Monday through Friday. My weekends are my own." She remembered his earlier caveat. "Unless, of course, you sleep over somewhere on Friday night." She curled her lip, making sure he knew what she thought of *that*. Although, come to think of it, Wynn had never—so far—slept away from the apartment.

She stood in front of him. He had been pacing the living room. Or maybe not *pacing*. More like restless wandering.

He stopped to keep from running her over. "You could have stayed out later." His tone was snide.

If she didn't know better, she would say he was jealous. But that made no sense. If it hadn't been for the funeral and the baby, Wynn would not have been spending time with Felicity at all.

She opened her mouth, but before she could respond to his snarky remark, her phone rang. "I need to answer this," she said, forgetting all about her spat with Wynn. "It's a Florida number. Might be my dad or my uncle."

When she answered the phone and heard her uncle's voice rush into a clumsy explanation, her world stopped.

Her responses were limited to "uh-huh. Uh-huh." And "thanks for letting me know." As she hit the button to end the call, the weirdest emotions strangled her. She wanted to cry, but she was frozen from the inside out.

Wynn came closer, his expression concerned. "What is it, Fliss?"

She stared at him, her lips numb. "My father died."

Then she burst into tears.

Wynn pulled her into his arms and held her tightly as she sobbed. He was a bulwark in a storm that had struck out of nowhere—without any warning at all. Afterward, she couldn't have said how long she cried. It might have been ten minutes or half an hour. The ugly, painful emotions ripped at her and left her feeling like a little girl lost in the scary woods.

All the while, Wynn stroked her back, murmuring words of comfort. Finally, when she was calmer, he left her long enough to get a damp washcloth for her face. She glanced in a mirror on the wall and winced.

Her eyes were swollen, and her mascara made tracks on her cheeks.

When she had cleaned her face, he perched on the arm of the sofa. "What happened to him?"

Felicity took a hiccupping breath, twisting the washcloth in her hands. "That was my uncle Danny. He and my father went fishing this morning. They had a good day. On the way back, Daddy spotted a huge grouper in shallow water. He threw in a line, hooked the fish and started reeling it in. But he collapsed."

"Was there any help?"

"Yes. They were close to shore. The EMTs responded to my uncle's 911 call immediately. But they assume it was a massive heart attack."

"I'm so sorry, Fliss."

His sympathy was too painful. The tears started again. "He was only sixty-three years old," she whispered.

"I know," Wynn said. And he held her again…

This time, she pulled herself out of the pit a little quicker, wiping her face with the back of her hand. "Sorry," she said. "I'll buy you a new shirt. Snot and mascara aren't a good look on you."

Wynn snorted out a surprised laugh. Then his expression gentled. He brushed the hair from her hot cheeks. "Go put on your pajamas and come to my room," he said. "I remember what it felt like the day I got the call about Shandy. You don't need to be alone tonight."

She looked up at him, her bottom lip wobbling. "Oh, Wynn. Were *you* alone that night?"

He nodded slowly. "Yes. I was."

When she didn't move, he took her by the hand and led her down the hall. "You're in shock, baby. Try to breathe. Do you want something to drink? A shot of Scotch might help."

"No, thank you," she said. "I'll be there shortly."

She left him standing in the hall and shut the door in his face.

If she'd been stronger, she might have been able to say no to his offer, but she felt like a star imploding, a dark hole swallowing everything that was light. The feeling was terrifying. She was an orphan now. An adult orphan.

Unfastening zippers and buttons was hard. Her hands weren't coordinated. Finally, she was done. She tossed her clothes on the bed and went into the bathroom to take a quick shower. She had washed her hair that morning, so it took less than five minutes to get clean.

After drying off, she went through her suitcase and looked in drawers for what she needed. Because it was heading into winter, and because she had been moving from Tennessee to New York, she had packed lots of extras, including her *comfy* pajamas, the ones she wore when the temperatures were cold—those nights when she came in from work and hadn't warmed the house.

The top and bottoms were old and thin from many washings. But the pale lavender flannel was so soft. Once upon a time, it had been covered in pink hearts. The design had mostly faded now.

When she looked in the mirror to brush her hair, she winced. Intimacy wouldn't be a problem tonight. She looked like the least attractive woman on the planet.

She found a pair of gray wool socks and put them on, hoping her feet would thaw. It wasn't cold in the apartment, but she was shivering.

In Wynn's bedroom, the covers had been turned back on his king-size bed. It was clear that he slept on the left side. She saw his book and his watch on the nightstand. So she climbed in on the right.

The shaking was worse now. She curled into a ball and wrapped her arms around her knees.

Wynn came out of the bathroom wearing navy knit sleep pants and a soft white T-shirt. His hair was tousled and damp.

He turned off the overhead light but left the lamp on the bedside table burning. When he slid under the covers, he reached for her. "Put your back against my chest," he said.

It never occurred to her to protest. Wynn's embrace

offered warmth and protection and a promise she wouldn't be alone for the next eight hours. "I'm sorry," she said, her teeth almost chattering.

"For what?"

She felt his breath on the back of her neck. "I can't stop shaking."

He rubbed her arm, the one he could reach. "I really think a tiny shot of Scotch would make you feel better."

"Okay, fine," she said. But inside, she protested silently when he left the bed.

He was back in no time, carrying a little glass. "Sit up," he said. "Can you hold this without spilling it?"

"I don't know."

"Scoot against the headboard."

Felicity was embarrassed. Her body was out of her control. She hated feeling this way.

Wynn sat on the edge of the bed and put the glass to her lips. "Drink it all at once if you can."

She put her hand over his, drew the glass to her lips, tossed back her head and swallowed the liquid in one rapid sequence. The alcohol burned going down and set her stomach on fire. She choked and gasped. "That's dreadful," she complained.

Wynn grinned. "Actually, it's not. Twenty-five-year-old whiskey from a centuries-old distillery in Scotland deserves respect."

"If you say so."

He took the empty glass and returned to his own side of the bed, climbing under the covers and spooning her as he had before.

Felicity hated to admit it, but the spreading warmth of the liquor was helping. That and Wynn's big body cradling hers. She closed her eyes, but she wasn't sleepy. Shock and disbelief made her weak and woozy, untethered to reality.

Wynn's big hand stroked her hair. "You're not asleep yet."

"No."

"You can talk to me, Fliss. I'll listen. And I won't try to fix everything. I'm told that's a masculine trait that drives women nuts."

His droll comment elicited a laugh. It was croaky, and she was surprised she *could* laugh in this situation, but the thought of Wynn trying to *evolve* was humorous.

She sighed. "It's not like we saw each other often," she said, "but I knew he was alive. On the planet. And we would talk and text a few times a month. He was my daddy. He raised me. All on his own, for the most part. I feel so guilty."

Wynn curled an arm around her, just below her breasts. "Then we're on the same page. I couldn't save my own sister. Talk about guilt."

"Yeah. I get that." Felicity was silent for several minutes, absorbing the peace of the odd situation. She would face hard days ahead. But right now, in this moment, things were okay. "Thank you," she said.

"For what?"

"For being here at the right time. It means a lot to me."

He pressed a kiss to her shoulder. "We go way back, Fliss. You're helping me with Ayla, and I'll support you through this. Now, go to sleep. The baby will be up at dawn whether we're ready for her or not."

It had been a very long time since Felicity had slept with a man—really *slept*. It was like falling into a cloud. She inhaled the familiar scent of Wynn's soap, reveled in the touch of his body against hers…and she slept. Deeply. Cathartically.

Sometime in the middle of the night, she woke up needing to pee. When she tried to climb out of bed, Wynn's arms tightened around her. "Don't go," he mumbled, clearly half-asleep.

"I'll be right back," she whispered.

She was gone hardly anytime at all. Yet Wynn snored softly when she returned. He had left the lamp on for her comfort. She turned it off before rounding the bed. Lifting the sheet and blanket with care, she reclaimed her original spot. Her groggy bedmate made a sound of approval and dragged her close again.

Felicity was shocked to feel his erection nestle in the cleft of her ass.

They were both fully clothed. Wynn was a virile man holding a woman. His response was natural, even in sleep.

But Felicity wasn't asleep at all. And she wanted him. So very much.

Maybe this was a need-to-affirm-life thing, but she felt her arousal build and build until she was literally unable to be still.

She eased onto her back. Now one of Wynn's legs trapped one of hers. He lay half on top of her, his face buried in the curve of her neck.

In the broad light of day, she might have talked herself out of this impulsive grab for comfort. But it was dark, and she'd been through a shock, and all she wanted was the sweet oblivion of sex. With Wynn.

"Wynn," she whispered. Even in this situation, the issue of consent was an ethical consideration. Besides, she wanted his full cooperation.

"Wynn…" She kissed the side of his cheek, felt the stubble and the hot skin. "Are you awake?"

He groaned. "I am now," he muttered.

"Make love to me," she whispered.

He froze, not a single muscle in his body moving. And now that he was fully awake, he had to know his body was ready to play.

Carefully, he eased onto his back, no longer touching her at all. "I don't think that's a good idea, Fliss. You're not thinking straight."

She cupped him through his sleep pants. "I don't want to think," she said. "I want to feel."

He grabbed her wrist and held her hand away from his body. "We're not going to do this," he said, the words rusty and low. "Go back to sleep."

"I can't. Besides, you probably knew this would happen when you asked me to come live with you."

"But not tonight. Not when you're lost and confused. I won't take advantage of you, Fliss." Wynn cursed under his breath, sat up and turned on the lamp. He raked both hands through his hair. "You're hurt and you're afraid. This is an impulse on your part. It doesn't take a shrink to see what's happening. Using sex to forget the world is a recipe for disaster."

"Maybe if I had picked up a guy at a bar. But not with you."

Wynn scrambled out of the bed, his expression hunted. "I need to check on the baby."

He disappeared with comical speed.

Felicity tried to analyze the situation. *Was* she being unfair to him? The poor man was trying to be a hero, a stand-up kind of guy.

She had to make this right.

Eight

Felicity tiptoed down the hall to Ayla's room. She stood in the doorway and watched as Wynn put his hand on the infant's forehead.

"Does she feel hot?" she whispered.

He turned to stare at her and then looked back at the child. "No. She's sleeping normally. And her skin is cool."

"Good."

When Wynn exited the room, he barely acknowledged Felicity at all. He stalked back to his bedroom. She wondered for half a second if he would try to keep her out.

But no...

He picked up his pillow and the book on the nightstand. "I think I should sleep on the sofa," he said. "The bed's all yours."

Her heart fell. "It's the pajamas, isn't it? I don't arouse you because I look like a frumpy bag lady."

"What in the hell are you talking about?"

"They're flannel. And they're old and ratty. Men like sexy lingerie."

A flush of dark color rode high on his cheekbones. The front of his sleep pants stuck out. "Wrong," he said tersely. "Men like naked skin. Always. Why do you think I made you put on pajamas in the first place? I'm trying to comfort you, Fliss. But you're not making it easy."

She crossed the room. "I'm sorry. I shouldn't have pushed you on this." She smiled wistfully. "My timing sucks. I get that." That was pretty much the story of their whole relationship. "I'm disappointed, but I understand. And of course, you're right."

He stood rigid, holding the pillow like a shield. "We can revisit this conversation later in the week. If you still want to talk about it. But not tonight."

He walked out of the room and closed the door behind him. Embarrassment washed over her, mixing with the grief and uncertainty.

She escaped to her room and flung herself into bed, drawing the covers completely over her body. In some tiny corner of her soul, she had believed that Wynn still had feelings for her. Not the kind to sustain a relationship, but at least enough to enjoy a hook-up for old time's sake. But if he did, his scruples were stronger.

She'd made a fool of herself. Wynn was trying to be kind. Earlier, he had intimated the two of them might enjoy a temporary affair.

But that was before she had rubbed snot on his shirt and turned into a needy crybaby.

She flinched when the light came on. At least it wasn't the overhead.

Someone pulled back the covers.

"Oh, for God's sake, Fliss. I know you're not asleep. I give up. Move over."

She sat up and glared at him. From the way he winced, she could tell that she must look absolutely wretched. "No, no, no. You made your stance on this issue perfectly clear. No sex when Felicity is a total mess."

He ignored her, sighed and joined her in the bed keeping a healthy distance between them. "We're both exhausted. The baby will be awake in a couple of hours. You need to sleep."

To her surprise, she did. It wasn't as nice as spooning with Wynn, but having him in her bed at all was the best feeling she could imagine at this low point in her life.

Wynn made her feel less alone.

When she woke up Monday morning, she *was* alone. But she could hear Wynn and Ayla in the kitchen. The sound of his deep voice and the baby's babbling carried down the hall.

And then it hit her. Wynn was supposed to be at work. She grabbed clothes but didn't bother with another shower. Once she was dressed, she brushed her hair and threw it up in a ponytail.

Makeup was no decision at all. A little colored lip gloss and that was it. She made it to the kitchen in fourteen minutes flat, almost skidding as she rounded the corner.

Wynn looked up in alarm. "What's wrong? Is the apartment on fire?"

"It's late. You need to be at work. And I know I'm leaving you in the lurch to go South for the funeral, but surely there's someone you know who could help out for a few days."

He grimaced. "That won't be necessary. I'm going with you to Florida. Ayla, too. We're your support group right now."

"But you—"

He held up his hand. "End of discussion."

She swallowed her pride. "Thank you, Wynn. I was dreading the thought of going alone."

"You're welcome."

Felicity tickled the baby's cheek. "How is she feeling?"

"Seems to be back to her normal self."

"I'm glad."

"When she goes down for a morning nap, I'll help you with whatever details I can."

"I need to call Uncle Danny again, but it sounded like a group of Dad's friends were putting something together...like a little memorial service. Maybe they're expecting me to bury him at Falcon's Notch. So I may not have much to do in Florida. Just attend, I guess?"

Wynn nodded. "We'll handle whatever it is. Get yourself some breakfast. I made waffles."

"You made waffles?" She raised both eyebrows.

"They're toaster waffles, smart-ass."

Felicity chuckled. "Ah. Now I get it."

By the time Felicity fixed her plate and poured coffee for herself, she found herself hyperaware of Wynn again. He looked tired, poor man. But that did nothing to detract from his wickedly sensual mouth or his beautifully masculine body.

Memories of the long night made Felicity sweat. It was demoralizing to admit that Wynn had done the right thing. She had been desperate to distract herself from what had happened.

If they'd had sex, Felicity would have been using Wynn. Even if he didn't mind, that didn't make it right.

Still, her body hummed with unfulfilled desire. The longer she stayed in New York, the more careful she would have to be. Last night could have changed things drastically.

"Wynn, I..."

He looked up from his plate and stared at her. "If this is about all the great sex we *didn't* have, forget it. You were in a bad place. We've moved on."

Felicity nodded slowly, but she wasn't convinced. If they had moved on, why was Wynn's knee bouncing underneath the table, and why did he keep looking at her when he thought she wouldn't see?

After breakfast, she went to her room and called her uncle. "I'm glad you were with him," she said. "And that he was doing something he loved. I'm glad he didn't die alone."

After another fifteen minutes with her usually laconic uncle, she was finally able to extract the details she needed. The service for her dad's friends would be at a local campground on Wednesday afternoon at 3 p.m. Her father had hated the idea of cremation. His body was being held at a local funeral home pending transport to Falcon's Notch.

"I'll be there for the service," Felicity said. "And I'll handle those other arrangements when I come."

After that, things happened quickly.

Felicity found Wynn in his home office. He was on a business call. The baby was asleep. When Wynn hung up, Felicity gave him the update. "The more I've thought about it, the more I think I should go on my own. Ayla has barely had time to adjust to her new environment. I don't see how you can leave her so soon."

"I told you," Wynn said. "She's going, too. That was my administrative assistant on the phone. Her college-age daughter is home on break for the holiday. Missy is an education major, early childhood. I've met her once before. She's willing to fly down with us and take care of the baby so you and I can do what we need to do."

"But it's Thanksgiving."

We'll have her home by noon on Thursday. Everyone's on board with this plan. Missy would have done this out of the goodness of her heart, but I'm going to pay for her spring semester as a thank-you."

"That's very generous."

He shrugged. "She's a great kid. And she's doing us a huge favor."

Felicity chewed her lip. "This is my crisis, not yours. I'm not going to fall apart. You can stay here and have Thanksgiving with your new daughter. Really. It's okay."

Wynn pulled her into his arms. "It's *not* okay," he said. "I want to be there with you."

"But why?" Her cheek rested over the steady thump of his heart.

"Because I care about you, Fliss. And because seeing you at Shandy's funeral and burial made all the difference for me. I couldn't believe you came. You were a shining light for me that day."

The kiss started out tender but heated up rapidly. It was broad daylight. They were both dressed. Nobody was talking about sex. But Felicity was *thinking* about it. A lot.

Wynn pressed her closer. His breathing was ragged. She clung to his shoulders.

The kiss deepened. For the first time, Felicity was afraid. Not of Wynn. Never him. But of the way he made her feel. Young and restless and eager to plunge headfirst into trouble.

The man smelled like syrup and pine forests. His solid, six-two frame dwarfed hers, sheltered her. Protected her.

She had been on her own for a very long time. Supporting herself. Doing all the grown-up things grown-ups do. Even her 401(k) was healthy.

But right now, she was tempted to throw away all the structure and security she had worked so hard to build. Because she wanted Wynn.

"I can't breathe," she said.

He let her go…but only so far. "Sorry, Fliss. You make me a little crazy."

She touched his chin, stroked his bottom lip. "At

the risk of getting shot down again, I should let you know I'm not feeling sad and weepy right now. Mostly, I'm just…"

His gaze sharpened. "Horny?"

Her face flamed. "And you're not?"

"Oh, I definitely am. In fact, I've wanted you ever since you set foot in my house in Falcon's Notch. We may be different people now, but our bodies recognize each other."

She shivered at the intensity in his voice and in his eyes. "Yes," she said simply.

"The baby might interrupt us." His warning was wry.

"Then I suppose we should quit wasting time."

Shock flared in his green eyes. "Hell, yeah." He glanced around him blankly, as if looking for inspiration. "Desk or bed?" he asked hoarsely.

She sucked in a shaky breath. "Do you keep condoms in your office?" she asked.

His disgruntled look might have been comical in other circumstances. "Bed it is."

He scooped up the baby monitor in one hand, took her wrist in the other and dragged her down the hallway to his bedroom, shutting the door quietly behind them. After putting the monitor on the dresser, he stared at Felicity.

Her nipples tightened, and heat coiled in her belly. She had never seen a man more intent on carnal pleasure. She cleared her throat. "To be clear," she said, "I don't expect this to be anything but recreational. I thought I should put that out there."

A slight frown put a crease between his eyebrows. "Duly noted. Are we done talking?"

Her cheeks were hot. "Yes."

Something happened then. Something inexplicable. Felicity felt paralyzed. It wasn't that she didn't want Wynn. She wanted him too much. The depth and breadth of everything she craved threatened to drown her.

Despite their joking about the baby's unpredictability, Wynn didn't rush. He unbuttoned her shirt so slowly she wanted to bat his hands away and do it herself. But she made herself watch.

Seeing his long, tanned fingers so close to her intimate flesh made all the air back up in her lungs. She forgot to breathe.

Gradually, he bared her to the waist and removed her shirt.

His gaze settled on her naked breasts. "Perfection," he said, his voice all low and rumbly. He touched her nipple with a single fingertip. Heat streaked through her body.

"Wynn…"

"What, Fliss?"

"Hurry. Please. I'm dying here."

His grin was pure wickedness. "Anticipation is part of the fun."

She dragged him close. "Not today."

When she kissed him wildly, he muttered a curse and lifted her off her feet. She was half-naked, but not naked enough. Suddenly, he set her down and they were grasping at snaps and buttons and zippers.

Wynn dragged her jeans and panties to her knees. She kicked out of them and helped pull his shirt over his head.

She got a little woozy at her first glimpse of his chest. The boy she once knew had turned into a honed, muscled, physically beautiful man, a man in every way. "I forgot how gorgeous you are," she said, as she pulled his head down for another kiss.

Wynn tumbled her backward onto the bed and came down on top of her. The skin stretched taut over his cheekbones. His eyes glittered with hunger. "I didn't forget anything."

He rolled aside long enough to grab protection from the bedside table and then came back to her. "I'd like to make this last, but I think we're working on borrowed time."

"Just do it," Felicity said. "Now."

Wynn moved between her legs, laughing at her. "Yes, ma'am."

She thought he would enter her quickly, but no. The diabolical man toyed with her emotions and her body, easing in slightly and withdrawing. She arched her back. "What are you trying to do?" she wailed.

His gaze bored into hers, as serious as a prayer. "Drive us both crazy," he whispered.

If that was his aim, it worked. He destroyed her. In ten minutes, he had her panting and whimpering and begging. Every time she thought he was ready for the main event, he hesitated, stroked, kissed.

Fire built in her belly and rose to her chest. Her breasts ached. Her sex clenched in endless yearning.

Wynn's face was all planes and angles, not a hint of humor or lightheartedness in sight now. His chest rose and fell with the force of his ragged breathing, but he maintained control.

That was something the younger Wynn hadn't mastered.

"I want you," she said, willing him to give her what she so desperately needed.

"How much?" he asked through gritted teeth.

She bit the side of his neck. "Enough to beg. Please, Mr. Oliver. I want your huge, beautiful—"

He slammed his mouth over hers, kissing her desperately. In the same instant, he penetrated deep, filling her so perfectly that tears wet her eyes. She blinked them away, not willing to miss a single nanosecond of pleasure.

Wynn's gaze went hazy. "Fliss," he groaned.

They were joined as one. Again. After fifteen long years.

But it was only sex.

She shoved the thought aside and lifted into his thrusts. The giddy rush of joy built and built and built until she cried out his name and climaxed in a rush of heat that burned away her reservations and left nothing but peace.

Nine

Felicity floated in a haze of dazed uncertainty. She had expected sex with Wynn to be fun. But *fun* was much too bland a word for what had transpired in this bed.

She might have been the one to *ask*, but Wynn had taken control and sent them both reeling into a place that was new. Adult pleasure. Based on a past relationship, but completely and utterly in the moment.

Breathless, and with her heart still racing, she inhaled carefully, pausing to enjoy the sensation of Wynn's big body pressing hers into the mattress. But soon, her smug happiness faded. He was so still, she began to worry.

She poked his tanned shoulder with one finger. "Are you asleep?" she whispered.

After several seconds of silence, Wynn lifted his head, gave her a wry look and kissed her nose. "No."

His dark shiny hair was rumpled. His skin was damp. He looked like the lead in an erotic movie.

"That was phenomenal," she said. "Admit it."

"Thank you." His lips twitched before he laid his head back on her shoulder. "I couldn't breathe there at the end," he complained.

"Not my problem. And besides, the phenomenal part was *us*," she clarified. "You can't take all the credit."

She felt awkward now, totally unprepared to exit the current situation. Where was a crying baby when you needed one?

Wynn yawned. "This parenting thing is hard."

Felicity snickered. "That was sex, not parenting."

"You know what I mean." He sat up and stretched, seemingly unconcerned by his nudity. When she turned on her side and drew the sheet to her chin, he slapped her bottom. "Playtime is over, Fliss."

She sighed. "I know. We've both got a million things to do."

His jaw firmed, and his eyes darkened. "Regrets?"

"No. You?"

He shook his slowly. "I think this was bound to happen sooner or later. I suppose the question now is what to do about it."

When he walked into the bathroom, Felicity scooped up her clothes and fled. She couldn't face him again. Not right now. Not when she didn't have an answer to his oblique question.

After a quick shower, she picked out black pants and

a crimson silk shirt. It was an outfit that bolstered her confidence. She needed that.

When she ventured out again, she heard Wynn in the nursery. Ayla had awakened from her long nap in a jolly mood.

Felicity decided she could use the baby to break the ice. So she stopped in the doorway and smiled. "Sounds like you two are having fun."

Wynn glanced over his shoulder and raised an eyebrow. "I didn't know we were dressing for lunch," he said.

"Very funny." Wynn was wearing the pair of sleep pants and T-shirt from last night. He must have heard the baby stir and hadn't had time to get fully dressed.

"I need to go out for a little while," she said. "Will you be okay with her? I won't be gone more than three hours."

Wynn scowled. "More socializing?"

"No. I need to buy a dress for the memorial service. Florida will be warm. I don't have anything suitable."

Wynn's expression softened. He propped Ayla on his shoulder. "I have a better idea. Let me call my friend Janeen."

"Janeen?"

"She's a department head at Bloomingdale's. I'll tell her what we need, and she'll send over a collection of dresses. You can try them on here. We'll send back whatever you don't want."

Felicity wrinkled her nose, disliking this Janeen woman already. "You dated her, right?"

His gaze was wary. "A million years ago, yes. She's now happily married to a captain in the NYPD."

"And she'll just *send* dresses to your home, no questions asked?"

"I'll have to give her a deposit on my platinum card, but yes."

Felicity swallowed her feelings of pique. The man had a past. So did she. And they weren't in a relationship. She nodded. "Then thank you. That would be great."

He held out the baby. "If you'll entertain this little one, I'll make arrangements for the jet."

"Isn't that expensive? We can fly my airline if I can get us on standby."

"With the baby, the private jet will be much more comfortable. And it will save time."

As he walked out of the nursery, Felicity shook her head in bemusement. It was hard to reconcile this suave, wealthy businessman with the wild, driven boy she had known in Falcon's Notch.

Was there anything left of the old Wynn Oliver? Or had he polished away all his rough edges in his rise to the top?

The shipment of dresses from Bloomingdale's arrived midafternoon. Because Ayla was napping, and Wynn was holed up in his office dealing with work stuff, Felicity took the boxes and bags to her room and locked the door. Not that she expected anyone to bother her, but just in case.

She stripped down to her bra and panties and took

the first dress out of the garment bag with the store's logo. Immediately she saw that letting Wynn have carte blanche had been a mistake.

These were no run-of-the-mill outfits. As she opened and examined every piece of clothing that had been sent over—including purses and shoes—she realized the dresses were designer pieces.

When she glanced at a few of the price tags, she felt faint. One of these was equal to eight months of her car payments. What was Wynn thinking?

Felicity couldn't in good conscience pay for any one of these without destroying her budget.

Even so, she tried them on. Wow. It was amazing what couture fashion did for a woman's self-esteem.

Her favorite was a sleeveless black sheath. The cut was deceptively simple. The fabric made the dress. The slubbed dupioni silk hugged her body in all the right places and was extremely elegant.

She put everything back in the original packaging, leaving out only the black silk. It was exactly what she wanted. But certainly not what she could afford. How was she going to tell Wynn that his effort to be helpful had bombed?

After changing back into her own clothes, she poured herself a cup of coffee in the kitchen and returned to her room to begin packing. For the second time, she looked through all the clothes she had brought to New York, including the boxes she'd had shipped.

There was only one black dress in the entire lot, and it had long sleeves. It would be miserably hot for

Florida. She really did need to go shopping, but how would she manage that without a confrontation?

She was almost done packing when Wynn showed up. Her door was open now. He surveyed the mess she had made. "Having trouble, Fliss?" His smile made her stomach do little cartwheels.

"I hate packing," she said.

"That must be a drawback for a flight attendant." His amusement made her flush.

"Packing for work is entirely different." She sighed. "How will they manage at your office with you being gone again?"

He shrugged. "It's a holiday week. You know how it is. Everyone's brain shuts down early. They'll be fine." He glanced at the stack of Bloomingdale's packages. "Did you find one you liked?"

She closed her carry-on and zipped it. "I appreciate you arranging all this, but I'll need to find something a little less..."

"A little less what?" He frowned.

Felicity stared at him. "Less expensive, Wynn," she said bluntly. "I can't afford any of these."

"I'll buy it for you."

His nonchalant words frustrated her. "No," she said. "That wouldn't be at all appropriate. If you don't need me between now and dinner, I'll make a quick shopping run. I know a couple of places where I can probably find the kind of dress I need without breaking the bank."

Wynn picked up the black silk sheath, the only one

she hadn't put back in its protective bag. "This one's nice," he said. "Did it fit?"

"Like a dream, but I'm serious, Wynn. It's out of my budget. You must have forgotten to tell your ex-girlfriend that I'm not in your league."

"What the hell does that mean?"

Was he deliberately being obtuse? "I have a good job and a nice home, Wynn, but you've made it to the big time. You fly around in private jets. You outfit your daughter's nursery as if she might grow up to be a princess. People jump to do your bidding. You're rich, and you're powerful. You and I don't move in the same circles anymore."

"So you're a snob."

She ground her teeth. "I need a different kind of dress."

He picked up the black silk, running his hand over the fabric like a caress. "Does this one look good on you?"

She nodded her head slowly. "*That* dress would look good on just about anybody."

"Then keep it. If it makes you feel better, I'll deduct it from your pay over the next nine months."

Felicity was torn. This new plan was better than letting Wynn buy her clothes. But it was still wildly impractical to spend so much. On the other hand, maybe if Wynn saw her in this beautiful frock, it would erase the memory of those awful lavender pajamas.

"Okay," she said. "I guess that will work. Thank you."

He put the dress back on the bed and approached

her with a look on his face that made her legs tremble. When he was in touching distance, he slid his hands under her hair and cupped her head, holding it steady as he went in for a long, thorough kiss.

Felicity put her hands on his wrists, clinging as the room kaleidoscoped in dizzying whirls. Wynn's taste was intoxicating. He held her confidently. There was no diffidence in his kiss, no second-guessing.

He staked a claim. And Felicity liked it. She kissed him back, not bothering to hide her enthusiasm. That cat was out of the bag. She and Wynn were physically compatible, and since neither was in a relationship, this resurrected attraction might follow a familiar path.

But she wasn't naive enough to see a future for the two of them. She still carried the weight of a guilty secret. One that might make Wynn look at her with anger and disgust.

It was an old secret, no longer relevant. But she had never told him one small detail because she had been ashamed. It hadn't mattered until now…now that they were sharing the same space, the same wild attraction.

Wynn pulled back, staring at her. "Where did you go, Fliss? You zoned out on me."

Her bottom lip threatened to tremble. "Sorry." She kissed him softly. "What are we doing, Wynn? Other than complicating our lives…"

"Having fun?"

His lopsided grin told her he wasn't taking anything between them too seriously. That was a good thing. Right?

Once again, she pondered whether she would have

to leave. But it seemed terrible to accept Wynn's help with her father's funeral and then bail on her job of caring for Ayla.

Any direction she turned, the choices weren't great.

"I should finish packing," she said, stepping back. "And do we have a dinner plan?"

Wynn stared at her as if he could see the turmoil in her brain. Then he sighed. "I do have a dinner plan. Missy is going to babysit Ayla this evening. A trial run for tomorrow's trip. You and I are going out to eat. We need a break. And you need cheering up."

"That's not necessary."

"Maybe not." He caressed her cheek with his thumb. "But I want to take a beautiful woman to dinner." Before she could stop him, he picked up the black dress again. "Wear this. The restaurant is fancy."

"But, Wynn…"

He was already gone.

Felicity hadn't realized how stressed she was… about everything. But by the time they were seated at a table for two with a white linen tablecloth and candlelight, she could feel herself mellowing.

The restaurant was lovely. Wynn's driver had picked them up at the apartment and dropped them off on a small side street near Central Park. From the outside, no one would guess how exquisite the establishment was, nor how exclusive.

From what Felicity could see at a glance, there were fifteen or twenty tables spread out over two rooms.

Each of the tables was tucked away in a small alcove, ensuring privacy on three sides.

"Wow," she said. "This is lovely."

"I'm glad you like it. The restaurant is new. It only opened last month. Word is still getting out."

"But clearly, you're the kind of man who can get a last-minute reservation at a spot like this?"

His gaze narrowed. "Are you complaining?"

She squirmed inwardly. "This is all commonplace to you, isn't it? The fancy cars and exclusive restaurants. The money-is-no-object shopping and the private jets?"

Green eyes turned to ice. "I've worked damn hard to get where I am today. I don't feel the need to apologize. Would you rather we leave? I'm sure there's a McDonald's somewhere we can patronize."

His sarcasm made Felicity feel petty. But she couldn't get past the change in him. Even though he had built a house in Falcon's Notch—and who knows why—he didn't fit in there anymore. This new Wynn Oliver belonged with the New York City elite.

She wasn't sure how she felt about that.

"I don't mean to criticize," she said carefully. "I'm sorry. I think I'm just having a hard time reconciling the teenager I knew with..." She waved her fingers. "With *you*."

His expression softened. He reached across the table and took one of her hands in his. "I'm still me, Fliss. You don't have to be afraid. I'm the same guy you knew in high school, just better dressed." He chuckled.

Felicity smiled, but she wasn't convinced. Wynn

had style and self-assurance. He possessed the careless confidence of the rich now. Swagger? Yes, he'd had that before. But the hint of bold masculinity was new.

"Thank you for bringing me," she said. Her tacit apology seemed to pacify him.

When the waiter arrived with heavy leather-bound menus, there were no prices on Felicity's. That was a first for her. She ordered a chicken dish and a savory appetizer platter. Wynn chose a steak with scalloped potatoes and a garden salad large enough to share.

The sommelier arrived with their choice of wine. The man tipped out a small portion, swirled the glass and handed it to Wynn. After Wynn's nod of approval, the dignified gentleman poured two servings in antique etched-glass goblets. Felicity began to feel like she was in a movie.

She was no stranger to nice restaurants. After all, she had traveled the world with her job. But this intimate *date* was over-the-top. Though she had dined at Michelin eateries, it was usually in the company of work colleagues. Her friends made the ambience entirely different.

She took a sip of her wine. It was the perfect blend of tart and sweet, rich and full-bodied. She was no wine connoisseur, but even she could tell this was an amazing bottle of vino.

"Do you like it?" Wynn asked. "I can ask for a bottle of white, too, since you ordered chicken."

"Those rules don't bother me. This is delicious." She finished her first glass and asked for a second.

As Wynn picked up the bottle with the French label

and poured, he gave her a questioning glance. "Why do I get the feeling you're working up the courage to say something?"

She swallowed, her cheeks flushing. That was the problem with someone who knew you very well. It was hard to dissemble.

No point in dragging it out. "I feel bad because you've been so kind to me yesterday and today, but I have to be honest, Wynn. I don't think I can take care of Ayla for a year. Or even nine months."

"Is the airline harassing you? I can speak to someone."

"It's not that."

He frowned. "So what's the problem?"

Maybe she should just lay it out there and see what happened. The wine had given her a nice little buzz... and a dollop of courage.

"I don't want to fall in love with you."

Ten

Total silence reigned for at least half a minute after her blurted truth bomb.

Wynn paled. Or at least she thought he did. It was hard to be sure in the restaurant's dim, romantic lighting.

The long, tanned fingers of his right hand drummed on the table. "Is that a possibility?" His jaw was tight.

"Well, what do you think?" she asked, exasperated. "We were together once. And do you ever look in the mirror?" She studied him now. The dark hand-tailored suit. Crisp white shirt. Patterned navy tie. He was sex on a stick. Looking at him made her weak. Add in their romantic past, and the situation became a potent minefield.

"I thought we were friends," he said, the tone oddly formal.

"We *are* friends. But I'm living in your house and kissing you and…" She trailed off, unable to mention what happened that morning.

"I thought you *wanted* us to sleep together," he said, narrowing his gaze so she felt like a witness in her own trial.

"I do. I did. But I think I made a mistake. You should find someone else to be your nanny."

"You agreed. We have a contract."

"I never signed anything, and you know it. My only sin is not saying no in the first place. It was an outlandish idea from the very beginning. You need a professional. A neutral party."

The meal arrived, and their conversation was shelved momentarily. But green eyes watched her, waiting as she ate.

Over the dessert course, he picked up the battle. "You're only saying the falling-in-love thing because you want to get back to your jet-set life and your *wide* circle of friends."

"Are you *trying* to be insulting?"

He snorted. "Be fair, Fliss. If you had seen a recent picture of me with two hot women hanging on my arm, wouldn't you have made assumptions?"

Her eyes widened. "Do you seriously believe I'm in the middle of some erotic ménage à trois?"

"Who knows?" He leaned back in his chair and licked whipped cream off his fork. "You could be sleeping with anybody at all, and I wouldn't know."

"Because we're strangers," she said forcefully, careful to keep her voice low. The waiters popped up with aggravating regularity. "We saw each other once on a plane, and then I came to your sister's funeral. We aren't even the same people we were fifteen years ago."

"I'm not sure that's true. You felt familiar in my bed, in my arms. Your kisses are the same."

Felicity didn't know how to respond because he was right. Being intimate with Wynn had been exciting and shocking and somewhat intimidating, but on another level, she felt comfortable with him. What an odd paradox.

"Maybe you're not wrong," she said grudgingly. "About the sex, I mean. But sex complicates things."

He snorted. "Says a woman. You won't ever hear a guy trot out that line. And when we're talking about sex with a lover you've known for years, it seems pretty damn easy to me. You and I always had something special in that department. Why can't we enjoy it? You're not going to fall in love with me…you don't even like me very much."

Her mouth fell open, and she blushed. "What does *that* mean?"

His smile gentled. He took the last bite of his French silk pie. "Finish your dessert, Fliss. It means you think I've sold out. You're not at all sure that having so much money is a good thing. I can see it in your eyes. You'd much rather I was a city employee or a school principal."

"That's ridiculous," she muttered.

"Is it?"

Unfortunately, he did know her all too well. They had both come from poor families. Seeing Wynn's world up close made her uneasy, though she wasn't sure why.

"We're getting off track," she said. "The point is, I need you to look for another nanny. As soon as possible."

He shrugged. "I don't want to," he said. "You're honest and trustworthy, and you love Ayla already."

"I'm not a Girl Scout," she snapped. "And I'm not so honest."

His gaze sharpened. "You're not?"

Well, shoot. Now she had to tell him the truth—didn't she? She shoved her dessert plate aside, unable to eat another bite of the rich chocolate. She was stuffed from dinner already.

This was the type of meal and the kind of place that catered to film stars and political icons. Trust fund babies and hedge fund managers.

Not for girls whose fathers couldn't afford field trip fees and patent leather shoes at Christmas.

She used the tines of her fork to draw random patterns on the tablecloth…anything to avoid drowning in jade eyes. "When we were together…in high school…" She swallowed, her throat tight. "It's true that I didn't know I was pregnant. I didn't lie about that."

"But?" He frowned.

"I wanted to be," she said baldly. "Sometimes when we had sex, you couldn't afford condoms, so we took chances. Every one of those times, I hoped the statistics would catch up with us. It's dumb, I know. Because we both wanted to see the world. But I also desperately wanted to have a baby with you."

Wynn loosened his tie as if he couldn't breathe. "You never told me that."

"I know. And then when I lost the pregnancy, I thought the universe was punishing me for being so stupid. So I'm sorry, Wynn. Sorry I lied by omission. If I had been honest with you about what I wanted, maybe things could have turned out differently."

He shook his head slowly. "You know that's not true. You said it yourself. Women have miscarriages all the time."

"Yes. But what I was really scared of was finding out you didn't want a baby with me. So I never told you the truth."

After that, Wynn fell silent. Maybe it was because the waiter brought the check, or maybe she had given Wynn a lot to think about.

When they stepped outside, the air was cold and damp, seeded with tiny pellets of ice. The car was still a block away. Wynn took off his jacket and wrapped it around her. She had left her heavy coat in the back seat because it was easier than juggling it.

Wynn put his arm around her as the sleet increased. "Sorry, Fliss. He got caught in the theater crowd."

"I'm fine." The truth was, she could have stood there all night with Wynn's warm body protecting hers. The cold wasn't cold, and the dark wasn't dark.

They didn't speak on the way home. Perhaps because the driver could hear every word. Wynn chatted with his employee briefly, but not to Fliss. She wanted badly to know what he was thinking.

In the elevator at Wynn's building, Felicity stared at the polished floor, but only after she caught a glimpse of herself in the mirrored wall. Beside Wynn, she looked small and defenseless. The beautiful black dress accentuated their differences—Felicity pale and blond, Wynn dark-headed and brooding.

Fortunately, there was a third party to break the ice when they got upstairs. Missy was a delightful young woman. She'd been able to put Ayla down for the night without any problems.

Felicity kicked off her high heels and draped Wynn's suit jacket over an armchair while Wynn walked Missy downstairs. The driver was waiting to take the babysitter to her home a few miles away.

It would have been easy for Felicity to hide out in her bedroom, but she had to know tomorrow's details, so she waited for Wynn to return.

When he entered the apartment, he gave her an odd look. "I didn't expect to see you," he said.

"Thank you for dinner. It was amazing."

"So polite," he mocked. "Is that all you want to say?"

"I waited for you because I don't know what time we're leaving tomorrow."

"Ah." He removed his tie and sprawled in a chair. "We'll need to head for the airport at noon. I've ordered boxed lunches for the flight. After you forwarded me the email from your uncle, I booked us rooms at a decent hotel in the general area. Would you mind packing for the baby in the morning? I need to go to the office for a short meeting, but I'll be back in plenty of time."

"Of course not."

He stared at her. "We're not going to solve all our problems in one evening. I promise you I'll think about what you said. What if we make a pact to survive the next several days, and then we'll talk?"

Felicity thought about it. Sitting through her father's service was going to be hard. Wynn was probably right. "That's fair," she said.

"Would you like a glass of wine before you go to bed?"

Wynn's deep voice infused the words with sensual overtones. Or maybe that was her overactive libido chiming in. She was still standing, unwilling to be drawn into an intimate late-evening interlude. "No, thanks. I'll see you in the morning."

He rose to his feet and crossed the room. When he caught her wrist in a light grasp, she stopped. His touch on her skin made a shiver roll through her body. "One more thing, Fliss."

She eyed him warily. "Yes?"

His thumb rested over her thundering pulse. "I've promised to think about finding a replacement so you can leave New York. But it seems only fair that you give some thought to staying."

"Staying?" She parroted the word.

"Staying," he said softly. "I think we could make it work for nine months."

His time frame was clear. She stared at him—those

sculpted masculine lips. The late-night stubble on his firm jaw. His mesmerizing eyes.

He was wrong. For Felicity to remain under Wynn's roof would be to howl at the moon so far out of reach. She needed to get away. She *had* to get away. "Fine," she said. "I'll think about it." But she wouldn't change her mind. The stakes were too high.

By the time they were airborne Tuesday, Felicity was a nervous wreck. Maybe the memorial service wouldn't be so bad. She could probably sit back and let her father's friends take charge.

But she still had to deal with the funeral home. And her father's final trip back to Falcon's Notch.

Missy was playing with the baby. Wynn was on his computer doing work. Felicity sat in the back row—alone—with too much time to think.

When they landed at a small airport near her uncle's home—and by default, her father's as well—Wynn had arranged for two cars to pick them up. The three adults and baby in one, and all their gear in the second vehicle.

The hotel was a generic chain, but on the high end. Missy spoke up when they were unloading. "I'll be happy to keep Ayla in my room tonight so you two can rest. I know that funerals are stressful."

Felicity saw Wynn freeze momentarily. She knew his plan had been to keep the baby with him and that Felicity and Missy would share.

When Missy walked toward the building, carrying

the baby, Wynn shot Felicity a guarded glance. "I can get a third room," he said.

Her stomach wobbled. "That might be best."

Something flashed in his eyes. Disappointment? Hard to tell.

Half an hour later, everyone was tucked away in their own rooms. Missy was giving the baby a very short nap before dinner. She said she would rather order pizza than go out.

That left Wynn and Felicity to fend for themselves.

They were staying in a small, semirural town off the beaten path. Too far from Disney to be popular, but still with a healthy population of tourists.

When a knock sounded, she checked the peephole and opened the dead bolt. "What's up?" she asked.

Wynn leaned against the door frame, looking suave and tempting. "I thought you might want to check out the campground where we'll be tomorrow and then maybe find a restaurant for dinner."

"It will be a far cry from last night's meal," she warned.

He smiled. "I get that. But since I spent most of my formative years living off Vienna sausages and boxed mac and cheese, I think I can handle it."

"Okay. Don't say I didn't warn you."

Wynn texted Missy to make sure she and the baby were okay. Then he was ready to go. One of the cars he ordered had been left behind for their use.

Felicity climbed into the passenger seat. She and Wynn had both changed into jeans and casual shirts.

Even in November, the humidity was noticeable. "Eat first or scouting first?" she asked.

"Let's find the memorial site. I've got the directions pulled up on my phone."

The Sleeping Pines campground was about as exciting as its name implied. About half of the spots were empty. The others were occupied by a wide variety of vehicles, everything from teardrop campers to fifth wheels.

As they drove through the entrance, Felicity spotted a small paper sign that said, "Vance Memorial Service 3PM." Suddenly, her father's death was all too real. The wave of grief was something she was learning to expect and accept.

Without saying a word, Wynn reached out and squeezed her hand. Her fingers clung to his for a moment, and then she released him. While she appreciated his support, leaning on Wynn when she was planning to abandon him and his daughter seemed wrong.

At the back of the property, they found a clearing with a large fire circle and a double ring of wooden bench seats. The ground was thick with pine needles. This area was clearly used for social events.

Felicity grimaced. "I think my black dress is going to be over-the-top."

Wynn shot her a rueful glance. "Maybe. But on the other hand, you'll be the closest family member in attendance, so it wouldn't be entirely unexpected if your outfit was more formal."

"I suppose." Her stomach growled audibly.

Wynn laughed. "I'd better feed you an early dinner before you get hangry. That's a real word now, isn't it?"

She nodded. "I love how pop culture can invent something so descriptive, and we all know what it means."

They ended up at a small seafood restaurant. From the outside, the rough-planked, one-story building didn't inspire confidence. But the hush puppies and shrimp were perfection.

They had almost finished eating when Wynn got a text. He glanced at his watch. "Missy has Ayla in the stroller and is walking her around the parking lot. I need to get back so I can play with her before bedtime."

"Of course," Felicity said. Awkwardness bloomed. With Missy along for this trip, Felicity felt superfluous. "Is there anything I can do to help tonight...with the baby, I mean?"

Wynn's eyes were on the road, his profile barely visible in the fading light. "Thanks for offering, but I think we've got it covered." He shot her a glance. "You need to relax. Tomorrow will take a lot out of you."

He was speaking from experience. She knew that. And though he hid it well, his emotional stress was probably still a factor now that he faced raising Shandy's baby.

At the hotel, she said a quick good-night and escaped to her room.

Once inside, the four beige walls mocked her. She dreaded tomorrow, plain and simple. Especially the trip to the funeral home, where she would be required to view her father's body.

She hated this experience, all of it, especially the fact that she wanted to lean on Wynn. He was not going to be a long-term part of her life, so she might as well keep clear boundaries.

After showering and washing and drying her hair, she touched up her manicure and tried to watch something on TV. But it was useless. She lay on the uncomfortable mattress and stared at the ceiling.

She felt buzzed, not anywhere close to being sleepy.

She was scared about tomorrow…

She missed Wynn…

At midnight, she still hadn't nodded off. At twelve fifteen, her phone vibrated. It was a text from Wynn.

I can't sleep…

She stared at the message, wondering how to respond. If she didn't answer, he would assume she was asleep. But she wasn't asleep.

A great chasm of uncertainty opened at her feet. If she crossed this line, she would be telling him she was available for his pleasure and hers. Was she prepared to do that? Knowing that she planned to leave him sooner than later?

Her ivory silk gown was far more flattering than flannel pajamas. And tonight, Wynn's focus wouldn't be about comforting her. This would be a round of mutually satisfying sex.

Her heartbeat sped up enough to make her shaky.

Her hands and feet were cold, though the room was warm. Her nipples pebbled against the bodice of her gown.

She looked at her phone, trying to decipher the layers of unspoken communication.

Finally, she got out of bed and crossed the room. With one flick of her hand, she turned the dead bolt. And then she hit Reply.

My door is unlocked...

Eleven

Wynn walked into Felicity's hotel room wearing nothing but a pair of sleep pants. His chest was bare.

She quickly retreated to the bed, her back propped against the headboard, the covers pulled modestly to her waist.

"Hey," Wynn said.

"Hey, yourself."

His eyes were heavy-lidded. "May I?" He indicated the opposite side of the king-size bed.

"Be my guest." When he mimicked her position, she shifted so she could look at him. "Why can't you sleep?"

Wynn's stormy gaze shot fire at her. "Why do you think?"

She swallowed. "Me?"

His chuckle held no real amusement. "Yeah." He

folded his arms across his chest. "In the spirit of this new honesty thing, I have something to say."

"Go for it," she said, but she braced herself.

His jaw jutted. "When we were together in high school, things ended badly. That was a very dark time in my life. You hurt me, Fliss, and in some ways, I never entirely got over it. I already had trust issues because of my parents, and then you rejected me—the girl who claimed she loved me more than anything. It messed me up. I haven't done well with relationships in my life, so I try to be honest with women and tell them sex is all I have to offer."

Her chest hurt. Tears stung her eyes. "I see."

"I hope you do. Because I can't be that eighteen-year-old guy with his heart on his sleeve again. I won't. Regardless of what we decide about you and Ayla, I want you, Fliss. All day, every day. All night, every night. Whenever you want me in return. I'll worship your body and give you every ounce of pleasure I can."

She had to force words from a tight throat. "Seems like a decent offer."

"I'm serious," he said. "I think you were kidding about the falling-in-love thing, but here's the bottom line. I don't do forever."

His words stung. "What about Ayla?"

"That's different. Completely."

"Okay."

"Okay, what?"

"I accept your terms," she said. "I want to have sex with you. Until I leave."

He frowned. "But you promised to reconsider."

"And you promised to look for another nanny."

"So we're at a stalemate." His voice was grumpy.

She scooted to the center of the bed. "Not when it comes to sex."

His mouth dropped open briefly before his eyes flared with heat and he met her in the middle. "I can live with that."

He dragged her closer, sliding his hands into her hair and kissing her wildly. There was no warm-up this time. His body was big and hungry, and his kiss brooked no opposition. Not that she offered any. Felicity wanted this. She wouldn't kid herself.

She wrapped her arms around his neck and felt his hot, smooth skin beneath her fingertips. "I'm glad you couldn't sleep," she whispered. "Very glad."

"Me, too." He ran his hands from her hips up to her waist. "I like this silky thing, but let's get rid of it."

She lifted her arms and held her breath when he drew it off over her head. He stared at her bare body for long seconds.

"What?" she asked, feeling more exposed and vulnerable than she ever had in her life.

"I can't explain it," he muttered. "You look the same, but different. Lusher, more blatantly feminine."

"Fatter?" she teased.

He didn't smile. "More enticing."

Her chest rose and fell when he touched her breasts lightly. The fact that her body responded visibly to his caress meant she couldn't hide from him. If she wanted to be intimate with Wynn Oliver, there was a certain amount of necessary risk.

It was her turn to explore his chest, and she took her time. Running her hands from his shoulders to his flat belly made her breathless. His body was at its peak. Taut, hard, primed.

When he smiled tightly and lowered her to her back, she sucked in a startled breath. This was really happening again.

But Wynn didn't do forever.

She tried to ignore the nagging reminder. It wasn't as if she had any notion of resurrecting their teenage relationship. Even so, a frisson of unease slithered through her veins.

Maybe Wynn thought she wasn't serious, but it was true. She was afraid of falling for him again. She simply couldn't let that happen.

He reached in the pocket of his sleep pants and dropped a trio of condoms on the bedside table.

Felicity's eyes widened. "Three?"

He shrugged, his gaze a mix of defiance and naughty charm. "You never know."

She closed her eyes when he leaned over her and sucked gently on her breasts, one at a time. Heat streaked through her body like lightning. "Wynn," she murmured.

"Hmm?" He lifted his head, his gaze slightly unfocused. "Was that a question, baby?"

"No." She shook her head slowly, her fingers grabbing folds of the sheet as he moved lower, kissing her very intimately. Her first orgasm slammed into her as she cried out his name.

His tight grin held a hint of smugness. "I'm just getting started," he promised.

"But you're still dressed."

"Insurance."

He covered every centimeter of her body, his focus unwavering. It was clear he enjoyed his work.

At last, he returned to her lips. "Sweet Fliss," he said, sliding his tongue deep in her mouth and using his hand to pleasure her elsewhere.

The second climax was better than the first.

The sensations were too much. She felt giddy and sated, greedy and relaxed. He played with her body as if he had all the time in the world.

But finally, she took control. She palmed him through his pants. "Get rid of these," she said, her breathing uneven.

"Gladly." He rolled to his feet and stripped off the sleep pants. His sex was rigid and full.

When he came back to her, he reclined on his side. She stroked the length of him, loving the way his chest rose and fell rapidly...the way his eyelids drifted shut as hot color flushed his cheekbones.

He didn't stop her when she kissed his lips and held his sex at the same time, moving her hand slowly. "Hell, Fliss..." He groaned as if she was torturing him. But his sharp breaths and restless movements told her she had only so much further she could go.

Finally, he rolled away from her, sat up and donned a condom. "How do you want me?"

The question surprised her. She had been expecting him to take control again. "I get to choose?" She grinned, loving the way he looked—wild and fierce and not at all sophisticated.

He sat back on his haunches. "Only if you make up your mind in the next ten seconds." The words were dead serious in tone.

"Me on top," she whispered.

His eyes flashed heat. "Yes, ma'am."

He sprawled on his back and took her by the waist as she straddled him. From there it was only a matter of heartbeats and ragged breaths to join their bodies.

Wynn watched her as he thrust deep. She felt starved for oxygen. The pleasure was intense, bordering on discomfort. Why had she thought she could handle this? He was too much in every way.

Because she could see the joining of their bodies and the way his chest heaved as he focused his attention on giving them both what they wanted, the moment was even more intense.

"I missed you," she whispered. "Every day for months and months."

His mouth tightened. "Don't say that. I don't want to know."

The sharp rebuke confused her.

Suddenly, Wynn rolled and put her beneath him, his expression tight with concentration and arousal. "You're going to come for me again, Fliss." He covered her mouth with his hand. "But I don't know how soundproof these walls are."

The command and the way he muffled her voice

sent her over the edge. Just as he hammered into her and groaned in release, Felicity came for the third time, her body reaching and reaching and shattering into boneless joy.

They dozed for an hour, entwined in an embrace of arms and legs and damp skin. When Felicity roused from her catnap, she lay very still and tried to memorize the perfect moment. There wouldn't be many of these, that much she knew.

When she saw the time, she shook his shoulder. "You should go back to your room," she whispered. "Before anyone sees."

"I know," he said. The two words were filled with grumpy, sleepy, masculine displeasure.

He kissed her throat, moved to her lips and totally destroyed her with what felt like tenderness.

But that was only a mirage. Tenderness was something a man and a woman exchanged in a *forever* relationship. Wynn Oliver didn't do forever.

He muttered as he found his sleep pants and donned them. After picking up the two condoms, he waved them in the air. "Cheated," he said. He tucked them in his pocket. "I was cheated."

She stood and wrapped her arms around his neck, loving the way he palmed her bottom and held her close. "Good night, Wynn," she said.

His sex was already at attention. "Good night, Fliss." He kissed her temple and released her.

As he walked to the door, she had to stifle the urge to call him back. She wasn't ready to let him go.

* * *

Wednesday morning was not pleasant.

It started out nice. Wynn and Missy and the baby came to Felicity's room at eight thirty for room service. The adults played with Ayla on the big bed. Missy answered questions about her college experiences and her future plans.

It was fun and relaxed and perfectly normal.

But eventually, Felicity had to face her responsibilities.

After Missy left to put the baby down for a morning nap, Wynn stretched and rotated his head on his neck. He groaned. "I could use more sleep."

Felicity smiled. "Me, too, but I don't mind."

He sobered. "Are you ready to go?"

They had an appointment at the funeral home at ten thirty.

She wrinkled her nose. "Not really. I've attended funeral services over the years to support friends and colleagues, but I usually pop in and out."

"Is that why you didn't go through the receiving line when Shandy died?" His gaze was curious, not judgmental.

"No. *That* was because I didn't want to talk to you face-to-face. Especially not with a hundred other people listening."

"This will be different," he said. "But I'll be with you. We can make it quick."

She sucked in a breath, wishing she hadn't eaten breakfast at all. "Okay. Let me brush my teeth, and I'll be ready."

Wynn nodded. "I'll grab the keys and be right back."

* * *

The funeral home was a low building with minimal landscaping and a white cross on top. The place might have been a pizza chain at one time.

It wasn't what Felicity would have chosen, but Uncle Larry had told the authorities to bring his brother's body here, so that was that.

Felicity didn't want to get out of the car. "I don't want to cry again," she said, her hands twisting in her lap.

Wynn leaned toward her, rubbed his thumb over her cheek and kissed her. "It's going to be okay. I promise."

The funeral home director was professional, but pleasant. He led them to a small anteroom, indicated the casket with a wave of his hand and departed, giving them privacy.

Felicity gripped Wynn's hand as they walked across the ugly burgundy carpet. Seeing her father resolved some of her anxiety. Her stomach settled. "It looks like he's sleeping," she said, feeling a rush of relief.

"Yeah." Wynn sighed. "I'm sorry, Fliss. He loved you very much."

"He did his best, I think. I always knew he could have sent me to live with someone else when my mom abandoned us, but he didn't."

They didn't stay long. Five minutes tops. It was a relief to get back out into the hallway. The only thing left was to deal with the logistics of transporting the body to Falcon's Notch.

Wynn touched Felicity's hand. "Will you let me handle this?"

She looked up at him, seeing the concern in his gaze. "Thank you," she said. "I'd appreciate that."

They were done before eleven thirty. Outside, Felicity sucked in a deep breath of clean air. "This was the worst part, I think. Maybe the service won't be so bad."

Wynn nodded. "You ready for lunch? I thought we could pick up something and eat it in the car. There's a pretty lake nearby."

"Sounds good. But what about Missy?"

"She's going to order room service again. I have my credit card on file."

They ended up driving through a fast-food restaurant and ordering burgers and milkshakes and fries. Now that the first hurdle was over, Felicity was hungry. She had barely eaten any breakfast because her stomach had been in knots.

Wynn parked the car at an overlook and lowered the windows. They were the only people at this spot, but the lake was dotted with sailboats and other watercraft.

Wynn put the big order of fries between them to share. They ate in silence. Out of the corner of her eye, Felicity studied him. In his crisp blue dress shirt with the sleeves rolled up, no one could mistake him for anything other than a man who was accustomed to being the boss. His broad shoulders and air of command were part of who he was, not to mention his physical appeal.

"Did you like your time in the military?" she asked.

He snagged a fry. "I did. My life growing up had so little structure. In the navy, I was part of something larger than me. The opportunities were there…for the guys and gals who wanted to take them. I worked hard, and it paid off."

"Do you think you'll want more children one day?"

He raised an eyebrow. "That's a hard segue." He chuckled.

"Sorry. My brain is all over the map today. But the question stands."

"I doubt it." He stared out the window. "I'm getting older, and my life is full."

Inexplicable disappointment settled in her stomach. His answer meant he was serious about his aversion to long-lasting relationships.

Felicity *wanted* a family. So far, she hadn't met a man she could visualize as the father of her theoretical children. But maybe he was out there somewhere.

"Shouldn't we get back?" she said.

"Yep. I told Missy we'd spend time with Ayla and give her a break before we have to leave again."

The next few hours flew by. Soon, Felicity was putting on her beautiful black dress and fashioning her hair into a loose knot on the back of her head. She added pearl studs to her earlobes and a matching necklace. Instead of heels, she chose black flats that would be more comfortable in the outdoor setting.

When she looked in the mirror, her face was pale, but she felt at peace. It was nice that her father had friends who cared enough to do a memorial service. Maybe her uncle would introduce her to a few of them.

Wynn and Felicity arrived at the campground half an hour before the service, but people were already gathering. Uncle Danny greeted her with a hug, his leathery face wet with tears. "I'm sorry, Felicity. I wish I could have done something more."

"You were there with him," Felicity said, hugging him back. "That's what matters."

Oddly, her uncle didn't encourage chatting with the mourners. He led Felicity and Wynn to a spot on the front row. "We'll start in a few minutes," he said.

The service lasted just under an hour. Six people spoke, in seemingly random order. Felicity got the impression the eulogizers were folks who liked having an audience and liked her father. Anyone who had the urge to honor him was allowed to talk.

All the speeches carried a similar theme. Felicity's father had been a good guy who enjoyed helping people.

Finally, it was over. Now Uncle Danny did introduce Wynn and Felicity to their fellow mourners. She shook hands and murmured her thanks.

One woman hung back until the small crowd dissipated. She looked oddly familiar.

When she approached Felicity and Wynn at the end, she had a strange expression on her face. She was midsixties with bleached blond hair and a tattoo of a cocker spaniel on her upper arm. Her sleeveless top bared skin that had been baked in the Florida sun for decades. She wore faded cargo pants and flip-flops.

"Hey, Felicity," she said, her manner diffident. "I don't know how to tell you this, but I'm your mom."

Twelve

Felicity went cold and then hot. "Excuse me?" Had her father found a girlfriend in Florida and never told her? "You must have me confused with someone else."

Wynn's stance went rigid. He hovered at Felicity's elbow. His frown probably should have deterred the woman, but it didn't.

The blonde smiled apologetically, picking at a loose spot of polish on her fingernail. "Nope. I guess this comes as a shock."

"You're mistaken." Felicity's words were formal. "My mother is dead." It was what she had always assumed, but she had no proof.

"Sorry to burst your bubble. I'm still alive and kicking."

"This isn't funny," Felicity said. She desperately wanted to leave, but the woman was insistent.

"My name is Iris Vance. I was married to your daddy, but then me and his brother—your uncle—fell in love. The three of us knew that nobody in Falcon's Notch would approve of me switching brothers. And a little kid like you would be confused."

"I was three," Felicity said, her hands clenched at her sides.

Wynn put an arm around her shoulders protectively.

"Yeah, I know." The woman's eyes reddened. "I was a real bad mother, but I always loved you. When your daddy moved down here a few years back, me and Daniel and him got close. Not weird sex stuff. Just friends. But it helped a lot to know your daddy had forgiven me." She paused, swallowed. "Maybe one day you can, too."

Wynn stepped forward, his jaw set. "You'll have to excuse us, Ms. Vance. Felicity and I have to be going."

"Well, okay, but I—"

He cut her off with one flash of green-eyed fury. "That will be all. Goodbye."

Felicity moved through a cloud of disbelief and pain. All these years. All these years, and her mother wasn't dead. Her father had known. Apparently, the entire time.

In the car, Wynn turned on the AC and pointed the vents in her direction. "Breathe, Fliss. You're going to be okay."

She stared at him, her lips numb. "You don't know that. I may turn into a raving lunatic. Not at all suited to caring for your daughter. Be forewarned. There's no going back from this. You were right all along to have trust issues. Apparently, people lie. That's what they do." She turned her attention to the scenery flashing by. "People lie..."

Wynn let her be. Perhaps he knew intuitively that she was in no shape for a rational conversation. When they pulled up at the hotel, Felicity went inside, not even pausing to wait for Wynn.

She found Ayla and Missy in Missy's room. Felicity picked up the little girl and snuggled her, trying to ignore the scary, empty hole in her chest. Over the years, she had imagined a thousand reasons why her mother might have abandoned her husband and child.

Never once did Felicity land on *shack up with your brother-in-law.* And what the hell? Her father had just let it happen?

The worst part was, she couldn't even demand an explanation from her dad. He was dead. Gone. Where she couldn't reach him.

Wynn gave Missy the keys to the car so she could take a break for a couple of hours. When the door closed behind her, Wynn came to Felicity and the child and put his arms around both. "Talk to me, Fliss. Don't bottle it up."

She closed her eyes and sighed. "Nothing to say. If you don't mind, I think I'll go to my room now. I'm going to shower and get ready for bed."

He frowned. "It's not even six o'clock."

"And I don't care," she said flatly. "What time do we leave for the airport in the morning?"

"Eight."
"I'll be ready."

Felicity didn't remember much of the trip back to New York. She kept Wynn at a distance, using interactions with the baby and Missy as excuses not to talk to him.

Her brain function was a fog of white noise.

What now? Should she stay with Wynn in New York and care for Ayla? Should she return to her own apartment in Knoxville and go back to work with the airline?

Or maybe she should physically move to another state. Find a new job, a fresh start.

Knowing that her mother was alive ate away at her. All those years, little Felicity had yearned to be normal, to have a mom like her friends did.

And for what? So Iris Vance could betray her marriage vows and pursue her own happiness at the expense of husband and daughter?

No matter how Felicity parsed the information, she couldn't understand such callous behavior.

Eventually, the Statue of Liberty and the familiar harbor came into view. The city sprawled out with unapologetic grace and power.

Felicity would be lucky to have even an ounce of that chutzpah.

As promised, Wynn delivered Missy back to her family by noon on Thanksgiving Day. He and Felicity and the baby arrived at Wynn's apartment soon after.

Wynn's driver deposited their luggage in the foyer, accepted a nice holiday tip and departed.

The sudden silence echoed. Felicity clutched the baby. Wynn sighed.

"I'd like to take you out for dinner," he said, "but I can't ask anyone I know to babysit on Thanksgiving Day."

Felicity managed to smile. "No worries. I'm not really hungry."

"I can get us a pizza right now and then order a couple of turkey and dressing dinners for later. Is that okay?"

"Sure," she said. She was touched by how hard Wynn was trying to be supportive, but really, what did it matter? He wasn't her husband. Even so, despite the eventual outcome, she wanted to enjoy this time with him.

The day crawled by. Ayla was unusually fussy, perhaps picking up on the tension between the two adults. Felicity showered during the baby's afternoon nap and stayed in her own room until she heard Wynn and his daughter moving around again.

They decided to wait on dinner until Ayla was down for the night, so Wynn ordered the Thanksgiving meal to be delivered at eight o'clock.

He also suggested they dress for dinner. Felicity chose a black suit with a tailored jacket, pencil skirt, and a sleeveless, silky gold top. She applied makeup and let her shiny hair tumble over her shoulders in a mass of curls.

In the mirror, she saw a woman in control. But the reality was much different. She desperately wanted the blind release of sex with Wynn, a chance to forget.

That might make things worse in the long run, but she was tired of fighting her feelings.

They ate in the dining room. The meal was fantastic. Beautiful slices of turkey breast and half a dozen sides…including bread and dessert. She couldn't even begin to imagine how much it had cost. Everything about Wynn's home and his lifestyle was grand, luxurious. No expense spared.

By unspoken consent, they avoided any mention of the Florida trip. Wynn told her about a new idea he was working on to detect pilot impairment. Felicity shared that she had thought about applying to be an instructor in one of her airline's training programs.

They discussed books and movies and travel ideas.

It was all very civilized.

Things didn't get strained until they adjourned to the living room with a bottle of champagne. This wasn't really a celebratory kind of week, but Wynn had ordered the very expensive bubbly with the meal.

He popped the cork and poured two glasses.

Felicity tasted hers. "Wow, this is delicious."

"Glad you like it." He sat down in the seat adjacent to hers and smiled. "To better days ahead."

"I'll drink to that." She touched her glass to his. Recklessly, she downed half of the pale gold liquid.

Earlier, Wynn had started the gas logs. The room had warmed nicely. Felicity shed her jacket. Only then did she realize that her top matched her drink. When that realization made her giggle inwardly, she knew she needed to slow down. She set her glass on the coffee table.

Wynn had shed his jacket as well and loosened his tie. He sprawled in his armchair, his posture relaxed and unguarded. The crystal flute dangling from the fingers of one hand completed the picture of sophisticated masculinity.

He looked stunningly virile and sexy as hell.

Felicity lifted her chin. "I know you'll want to argue about this, but I plan to go to Falcon's Notch a week from Saturday and bury my father. I'll go alone. Leave Saturday morning and be back by Sunday evening."

When he started to protest, she held up her hand. "I don't want to hear it. Ayla, cute as she is, complicates things. It will be a private graveside service. No need for a big fuss."

His gaze narrowed. "Is it so very important for you to prove you don't need anyone?"

She firmed her resolve. "You and I are not in a relationship. My responsibilities are my own."

"And if we share a bed tonight...this week...what then?"

"Just sex," she said, the words deliberately flippant. "You've been clear about that, and I appreciate your honesty."

The irritated expression on his face spoke volumes. Wynn was a man who liked to control every situation. Right now, she was pissing him off.

"Travel is exhausting," he said. "It might be nice to have a friend along for the ride. I could get Missy to stay here with Ayla. Probably."

"Thank you," Felicity said...very politely. "But I'll be fine."

With his free hand, he clenched the arm of the chair, his knuckles white. "I wish I could be the man you need. A forever kind of man. But I'm not. For a dozen different reasons. But this isn't the time for you to make snap decisions. You have feelings to process."

She lifted an eyebrow. "You're not my shrink."

He sat up, leaned forward, set his glass on the table with hers. "No. I'm not," he said, jaw clenched. "I get that. But for God's sake, Fliss. You just found out that your mother isn't dead…and both of your parents lied to you. What are you going to do about that?"

"Nothing." She shrugged. "Or maybe I'll take a page out of your book."

His gaze narrowed. "Meaning what?"

"When you and I broke up, you ran far and fast from Falcon's Notch and reinvented yourself as a business tycoon. Look at you. No one in this city has any notion that you're the kid who came to school in dirty clothes because your parents couldn't be bothered to go to the laundromat."

His jaw hardened. "So?"

"How am I any different if I simply ignore what I found out in Florida?"

Green eyes blazed. "Your mother *isn't dead*. You have the chance to mend something."

"I don't want to," she snapped.

Wynn bowed his head and rubbed his temples. "Fine. Poison your guts with resentment and anger. Why should I care?"

She kicked off her shoes, curling her toes into the carpet. "I don't need your drama, Wynn. All I want is your body. Preferably naked, though you do look very fine in that suit."

He gaped at her.

Deep in her knot-filled stomach, she reveled in the fact that she had managed to shock him.

"Fliss, I—"

She glared. "If you dare tell me we can't have sex because I'm *not in a good place*, I may punch you."

His lips twitched in a wry smile. "That sounds interesting. Would I be tied up in this scenario?"

"In your dreams." She huffed out a laugh. "To be clear, I'm ready for bed. With you." She rose to her feet and stood in front of his chair, straddling his legs. "Is that a problem?"

His humor faded. "No. But who needs a bed?" Slowly, he put his hands on her thighs, just above her knees, and shimmied the thin crepe skirt upward. Now he could see her black thong…and the fact she was mostly naked from the waist down. "Holy hell," he muttered.

He pushed on her shoulders until she was seated on his lap, the skirt awkwardly bunched at her hips. He cupped her head in his hands and kissed her lightly. A butterfly caress on her lips.

She moaned and leaned closer. He was so warm and wonderful. Now that it was happening, all thoughts of using sex for oblivion faded. Her arousal sprang to life, surprisingly voracious.

Nipping his bottom lip with her teeth, she coaxed him toward the limits of control. "I don't want *care-*

ful tonight," she said. "Show me your wild side. Push us both to the edge."

His chest heaved. His face flushed. "Be careful what you ask for." He found the single button at the back of her neck, freed it, and lifted her top over her head. Her sheer black bra matched her panties. He paused to admire it, then worked on her skirt.

It frustrated them both when she had to stand up and step out of the skirt, but soon she was back in his lap, her arms curled around his neck. She was shaking, wanting, pleading.

She covered his face in kisses even as he squeezed her ass and groaned. "Don't make me wait," she moaned, leaning into him until he had to fall back in the chair.

He wrapped one arm around her waist, dragging her against his chest. "You drive me crazy," he said hoarsely. "I don't know how it happens."

She chuckled, running one hand through his thick, luxuriant hair. "It's because I know you. All of you. The same way you know me. It's dangerous, but it's good."

Wynn stared at her as if her words had struck a nerve. Maybe she shouldn't have been so honest. But it was true.

They had nothing to hide from each other. To Felicity, the blue-collar billionaire from Falcon's Notch was simply an ordinary man beneath his bespoke suits and expensive watches and shoes. Once upon a time, he had lain naked with Felicity in a grove of pine trees and made love with her under a harvest moon.

That sort of a thing stayed with a person, no matter how much wealth piled up in the bank.

The two of them were successful, but they could never escape their past, even if they wanted to...

He urged her to her feet. "I'm ready this time," he said, producing protection from his pants pocket.

She smiled. "I like that about you."

While she watched, he undressed quickly, without an ounce of self-consciousness. Felicity stood with her arms crossed. The less he wore, the more comfortable she felt in her two remaining items of clothing.

At last, his tall, broad, beautiful body was bare... completely.

Her nerves returned. His magnificence was a little overwhelming. That boy in the woods had been less intimidating.

He cocked his head, studying her face. "What's wrong, Fliss? Second thoughts?"

"Not at all." She swallowed, her throat dry. "I get nervous right about now. Every time."

Wynn picked her up. "Wrap your legs around my waist. Why, baby? What's there to be nervous about?"

She waved a hand. "I don't want to go back to the past. Not at all. But the old you was easier."

Now a small frown creased his forehead. "Easier?"

"I knew what you were thinking," she said. "What you wanted."

"I'm the same guy, Fliss, I swear."

"No," she said slowly. "I don't think you are. But it's all right. I like you anyway."

There was a wheeze in his ragged chuckle as he carried her a few steps across the room. "Your brain is a labyrinth," he said. "I hope we find our way back out."

"Where are we going?" she asked. "I thought you were in a big hurry."

"Oh, I am," he said, pinching her butt. "But you asked for wild and edgy. I aim to please."

"Wynn!" She gasped when he dropped her to her feet and bent her over the arm of the sofa. Before she could say a word, he had used his discarded necktie to secure her wrists over her head.

He groaned. "Damn, woman. What a view."

"I'm still wearing my bits and pieces," she pointed out.

"I know. Makes it erotic." He reached beneath her with both hands and caressed her nipples through the thin fabric of her bra. "This is what you asked for, my sweet. Standing on the edge." He put one hand in the small of her back and pressed. "Do you feel wild yet? Out of control?"

"Getting there," she muttered, breathing hard. She knew he was teasing her, but the game was working. She wiggled her bottom. "I'm ready, really ready. And the edge is plenty close."

"Patience," he whispered, the words silky with sensual threat. "We'll both go over together, I promise."

Thirteen

During her initial flight attendant classes, and in refresher courses, Felicity had taken a handful of self-defense modules. In the right circumstances, she had a decent chance of taking down a full-grown male adult.

But none of her on-the-job training had covered this situation.

She rested on her elbows with her fanny pressed up against Wynn's considerable *attributes*. By the sheer weight of his body and her submissive position, he was in control.

Her heart raced. Her sex was damp and needy.

Could she rear back, hook one foot behind his calf, and knock him to his butt? That might be fun. But she would have to catch him off guard.

While she was debating that tactic, Wynn leaned

forward and tucked her hair over one shoulder. Then he kissed the nape of her neck.

A hard shudder rippled its way from the damp spot at the top of her spine, all the way down her to her legs and below.

She went weak. Breathless.

Wynn compounded his torture by licking the same area inch by inch. She felt his tongue on her hot skin, heard his murmured words of praise, smelled the warm male scent of him surrounding her.

What she couldn't do was see.

Her elbows had given out. Now the side of her face pressed into the velvety sofa cushion.

Wynn took his time. He stroked her bottom, running his hands up and down the backs of her thighs.

"Wynn?" she said, trying to snag his attention.

"Mmm?"

"Will you let me up now? I want to touch you."

"You asked for the edge, Fliss. Remember?"

"I changed my mind." She was getting dizzy. "I'll settle for missionary position on a soft bed."

His low, amused laugh made the hair on her arms stand up. "I don't think so, darlin'. We've crossed the line. There's no goin' back."

For the first time, it occurred to her that in certain situations, Wynn's Southern accent was more pronounced. He must have worked to erase it in his professional life. But here and now, his slow-as-molasses drawl was sinfully rich and impertinent. As if he didn't give a flip about her opinions.

This game they played was getting more dangerous by the moment.

"I'm uncomfortable," she said, trying to sound sincere. "Let me up so I can kiss you."

He leaned over and nibbled her earlobe. "We'll get to that. Do you like it from behind? We never did that as teenagers. I wonder why?"

"Because we didn't have time for nuance," she snapped.

He laughed. "Well, hang on, Fliss. I'm going to nuance the heck out of you."

It sounded more like a threat than a promise.

She sucked in a sharp breath when she felt him drag her tiny panties down her legs.

"Lift your foot," he said. "Now the other one."

And just like that, even her faux modesty was gone.

Wynn palmed her sex. "You're ready for me, aren't you, sweet thing? Hot and slick and perfect."

He entered her with a single finger.

Felicity tried not to hyperventilate. "Don't make me come," she pleaded. "Not yet. Not without you inside me."

"I don't think you're in any position to issue demands. When a man and a woman go to the edge, anything can happen." Gently, he stroked the tiny spot that made her moan.

Wynn was pushing her closer and closer. And he knew it, damn him.

"Please," she begged. "Either let me go, or..."

He moved suddenly, crouching on the floor beside

her. His eyes glowed like molten emeralds. "Or what, Fliss?"

She was helpless when he kissed her. His lips were firm and warm, his tongue insistent as he probed her mouth.

"I want you," she said. "Now."

He broke the kiss and sat back on his haunches. "Wild and edgy. My choice."

She frowned. "Why do you get to pick?"

His smile made her toes curl against the carpet.

"Because I'm in charge tonight."

He moved to his original position. She heard a foil packet being torn open. Felt his fingers spreading her, readying her.

"Wynn..." She breathed his name in shock. Had she known he was going to call her bluff?

His sex was full and heavy. He penetrated her slowly. "Hang on, Fliss."

When she found the energy to rise onto her elbows again, the slight change in position drover him deeper.

They groaned in unison.

"Please don't ever stop," she said with all sincerity.

He leaned over and into her, his laugh hoarse and winded. "I'll do my best, baby."

Slowly, he made love to her. With his body if not with his heart.

In that instant, Felicity knew she was lost. Because she *was* in love with him. And it hurt. Like an old wound that had never healed.

She had gone on with her life. Had found meaning and purpose and happiness.

But nothing had ever been as good as this.

She knew it never would.

Wynn wrapped his hand in her hair. "Tell me you want me," he demanded. "Tell me now."

"I want you." That much she could give him. Not the other. Not her easily bruised heart.

He picked up the pace. Gripping her hips, he pounded into her until he gave a hoarse shout and came. Felicity groaned and found her release amidst his. Her climax was sharp and sweet, the ripples endless.

Eventually, their skin cooled.

Wynn muttered something unintelligible before leaning forward to untie her wrists. Then he helped her to her feet.

Felicity was mortified when she wobbled, and Wynn laughed.

He kissed her forehead. "You have the best ideas, Fliss."

She found her clothes and used them as a shield. "Good night, Wynn."

He frowned. "That's it? Good night?"

Was he looking for a critique of his performance? She made herself step forward casually and kiss him on the cheek. "I'll stay until the New Year," she said. "That should give you time to find my replacement."

His mouth set in a hard line of displeasure. "Explain to me again why you're dead set on leaving?"

"It's simple," she said. "I'm not getting any younger. I want a husband and a home and a family of my own one day. I need to get back to my job and my real life."

She had told him the truth about the past—that she

had wanted babies with him—and more recently, she had done him a favor in caring for Ayla until Wynn could gather his wits and get settled in New York with his new responsibility.

He scowled. "And do you already have a candidate in mind for this fairy-tale existence?"

"I do," she said slowly. "Plenty of them. Colleagues. Passengers. I'm lucky to meet a wide circle of people."

"I see." Now his features were set, his expression neutral.

"I realized I wasn't being fair to you," she said. "This would be a terrible time to search for a replacement nanny, with the holidays and all. So I'll stay until the first of the year. But don't think you can procrastinate. I won't change my mind. Come January, I'll be back on the flight deck."

"And you and me? In the meantime? Our sexual relationship?"

If she said no to intimacy, he might eventually guess she was in love with him, so she tried to make light of it. "I see no problem with that. We enjoy each other's company. And we're compatible in bed."

"Sounds like you have everything worked out." The words were tight, critical.

"Don't try to pick a fight," she said. "Let's enjoy the moment."

He sighed. "I suppose I don't have a choice. I can't chain you up here. If you have to go, I'll work something out."

"Thank you," she said, her heart breaking. "You and Ayla will be fine. I'm sure of it."

* * *

Nine days later, Felicity stood at the familiar cemetery in Falcon's Notch and watched her father's coffin being lowered into the ground. Her grief had run its course. Now she was numb.

Somewhere, her resentment and fury burned. But it seemed disrespectful to be angry with a man who could no longer defend himself, so she had chosen to bury her emotions and deal with practicalities.

Wynn had done his best to tag along. He'd offered the private jet for comfort and convenience. He'd sworn she would feel less alone with him by her side. Everything he said was true. But Felicity turned him down.

It was one thing to sleep in his bed every night. She couldn't let him take over her life.

After the brief graveside service, she drove back to Knoxville and opened up her apartment to air everything out. It was a nice place, but even before Wynn dropped back into her life, this little home hadn't held any emotional significance. It was her third or fourth apartment. Her memories and her friendships were what mattered.

She went from room to room, trying to imagine herself moving back here in January. This was a base, nothing more. Her assignments would take her all over the world.

As she climbed into bed that night, she tried not to think about Wynn. The thought of him in New York—with Ayla—tugged at her heart. The two of them were dear to her, but she had to find her own family.

It was clear now that Wynn would always hold a

piece of her heart. Even if she managed to find a compatible mate and start a relationship with him...even if he was a man who could give her what she wanted... would she ever get over loving Wynn...twice?

Her flight back to New York Sunday afternoon was uneventful. When the cab dropped her at Wynn's apartment and she went upstairs, she was surprised to see Missy.

The young woman smiled. "Hi, Ms. Vance. How was your trip?"

"It was fine." Missy and the baby were playing on a quilt on the living room floor. Felicity picked up Ayla and snuggled her. "Is Mr. Oliver out?"

"Yes, ma'am. He said he'll be back by ten."

"Do you come home from college every weekend?"

"Oh, no. But my mom's birthday is always a week or so after Thanksgiving. I don't want her to feel cheated, so I come back to celebrate her big day."

"That's sweet of you." Felicity tried to gather her scattered thoughts. "I can take Ayla now...so you can leave."

"Thanks, but I'm fine. Mr. Oliver said you'd had a tough weekend, and he didn't want you to have to come home and babysit. Why don't you relax and do whatever you need to do? I'll be here until he returns."

Felicity nodded, feeling oddly out of sorts. She was planning to leave Wynn's employ by the New Year. Why did she care if Missy stepped in? Maybe because Felicity had come to regard Ayla as her own. Reluctantly, she set the child back on the floor with her toys.

Missy had things under control, so a short while

later Felicity slipped out of the apartment and walked a block and a half to the small restaurant that had become her favorite. It was a mom-and-pop business that served up authentic Italian dishes. Felicity needed the comfort food tonight.

At a table for one with a single candle burning, she wondered what would happen if she told Wynn how she felt. If she brought up the possibility of starting over.

He had told her he wasn't interested in permanence with *any* woman. Was that the truth? Or was he protecting himself like she was? If she told him she was falling in love with him again, would it make a difference? A man could change his mind…right?

Deep down, she knew she was courting heartbreak.

Yet she couldn't abandon the notion that she and Wynn were two of a kind. That they were meant for each other.

On the walk home, she bent her head into the wind…shivering. As she passed the entrance of a posh clothing store—shuttered on a Sunday evening—she stepped into the small alcove for a reprieve from the cold and rubbed her hands together.

When she looked up, a couple on the opposite side of the street caught her attention. The woman was a redhead, tall and statuesque. The man was very familiar. It was Wynn.

As Felicity watched, the woman went up on her tiptoes and kissed him on the mouth. To be fair, Wynn didn't extend the kiss. He stepped back, laughing, and removed the woman's hands from his shoulders.

Felicity's stomach flopped unpleasantly.

She knew he had other relationships. But she had coaxed herself into believing otherwise. How stupid could she be?

As she watched from her darkened hiding place, Wynn hailed a cab, tucked the woman inside, then turned in the direction of his building and strode away, his dark hair ruffling in the breeze.

Felicity took her time walking back. When she arrived at the apartment and went upstairs, Missy was gone. Wynn was changing Ayla into her pajamas. Felicity lingered in the doorway of the nursery.

Wynn turned and smiled when he saw her. "There you are. Missy told me you had gone out for dinner."

"Yes. I didn't have lunch, so I was hungry."

Their prosaic conversation camouflaged a host of emotions. Felicity had missed him in the time she had been gone. After sharing his bed every night for more than a week, it had felt odd to sleep alone last night.

He finished snapping the baby's pajamas and picked her up. "We're glad you're back, aren't we, Little Bit?" He blew a raspberry on the infant's cheek, making her laugh.

Felicity's heart turned over in her chest. Here was everything she wanted. If things had turned out differently when she and Wynn were teenagers, they might have been a couple. Parents. Together.

She cleared her throat. Enough with the secrets and the lies. It was time for plain speaking. "I saw you," she said. "When I was walking back. You were with a woman."

His body language changed from relaxed and mellow to wary. "Yes. Gretchen and I had dinner. I owed her an explanation, and I hadn't found the opportunity before now."

"An explanation for what?"

He shrugged. "I ended things with her rather abruptly when Shandy died. Tonight, I explained that my life was taking another direction. I have Ayla now. She understood."

Felicity had her doubts about *Gretchen's* amiability. Any woman with even a slight claim on Wynn Oliver's affections wouldn't cede the field easily...even to a child. "That's nice for you," she said, noncommittally.

His gaze narrowed. "Are you jealous, Fliss?"

Inside she felt hollow and anxious, but she shook her head slowly. "I have no right to be jealous. Your life is your own."

"Even after our recent...escapades?"

Her cheeks flushed. "We agreed that was recreational."

"Ah," he said.

They went to the living room and played with the baby. This had become a ritual...a few moments of normalcy amidst the uncertainty of their sexual connection.

As usual, Felicity held back in the evenings. Wynn was the child's father. Felicity was only a babysitter.

When Ayla got fussy, Wynn stood to take her to her room. He gave Felicity a measured look. "Don't disappear," he said. "I want to talk to you about something."

After he left the room, Felicity stood and paced. She

was terrified of revealing that her feelings were more than physical. As a girl of eighteen, she had loved him. Now, back in his orbit, she understood that no other man would ever measure up.

Where did that leave her?

Finding out that Wynn had been out to dinner with *Gretchen* tonight had thrown Felicity off her game. It had reminded her that Wynn had many women in his life. How could Felicity ever have the guts to tell him how she felt?

She loved sharing his bed. But she wanted more. She wanted intimacy. Real intimacy. The kind of relationship where two people faced the world as a cohesive unit, bound by love. A couple who shared dreams and fears. And yes, incredible sex.

When Wynn returned, she was no closer to knowing how to handle him. So she chickened out. She told herself she needed more time to weigh the pros and cons of being completely honest about her feelings.

He sat in a chair and sighed, his expression torn. "Do you think she misses her mother?"

"How can I answer that? I'm sure she does. But what do I know about an infant's brain? You've given her love and stability. That's a lot, Wynn. She's a lucky little girl."

"Maybe…"

He made a visible effort to shake off his concerns. "I have a proposition for you," he said, his eyes twinkling.

"I'm afraid to ask."

Wynn chuckled. "Next Thursday night, one of

WynnSpeed's big marketing partners is holding a holiday party at a restored warehouse in Tribeca. It's going to be black tie, very glitzy. You and I have dealt with some hard times lately. What would you say to kicking up our heels and having fun?"

The image of Wynn Oliver kicking up his heels didn't compute. But the thought of going to a party with him—on a *date*—lifted her spirits.

"I could be persuaded," she said. "But I might need an afternoon to shop for a dress. I brought mostly casual clothes with me when I came to New York."

"Not a problem," he said. "And if you want to run anything by me, I'm sure we can arrange a private fashion showing."

"Are we talking about sex?" she asked, her nerves humming.

He glanced at the sofa, his grin wry. "It's pretty much all I think about since you let me tie you up."

"I didn't *let* you do anything," she said, laughing.

He sobered. "I want to be clear. I'm interested in having your body but it's far more than that. And to be honest, I'm not sure I like it. I find myself wanting to protect you. That's not something that happens with other women."

Fourteen

His words threatened to break her heart. "I don't need you to coddle me," she said flatly. "All I want to do is live in the moment."

He blinked, rubbed his face. "You make it hard for a man to take care of you, Fliss."

She went to him and curled up in his lap, resting her head on his shoulder. "I have no complaints. I like the way you turn me inside out so I can forget the world exists."

He sucked in a sharp breath when she unbuttoned the top few buttons of his shirt and found the warm skin underneath. "Is avoidance healthy?" he asked, the words strangled.

"I don't really care." She kissed his throat. "Make love to me, Wynn."

"Felicity, I—"

She put her hand over his mouth. "Less talk. More action."

He stared at her. "You're hurting, Fliss."

"No, I'm not." Avoidance was her new mantra. Avoid telling Wynn how she felt. Avoid dealing with her family.

"Baby, it's written on your face. You can't pretend your father's funeral never happened. Or that you didn't find out about your mother."

Slowly, she slid from his lap and onto her feet. "Not another word. I'll have sex with you, Wynn. In fact, I want to…very much. But you've made it clear that we are not in a relationship. So I don't need to hear your thoughts about my screwed-up family. It's a house of cards built on lies."

The front of his pants tented. He was aroused. He couldn't hide that. But still he tried to reach her. "They didn't set out to hurt you, Fliss. You were collateral damage. And I know they regretted it."

"Is that supposed to make me feel better?" The truth was no one in her life had loved her enough to be straight with her. Not her parents, who concocted an elaborate lie about her mother's disappearance. Not Wynn, who was too proud to tell her she had hurt him when she declined his impulsive marriage proposal. She had made her way from childhood to adulthood alone.

Unless she left New York and found a new love to wipe Wynn Oliver from her memory banks, she would always be alone.

She didn't want that. At all... But how could she possibly tell him the truth? How could she talk about love knowing how he felt about the future?

"I'm sorry," she said, summoning a smile. "I'm feeling a little fragile. But that has nothing to do with you and me. I'll deal with it."

He stood as well and took her hands in his, his grasp warm and firm. "You don't have to be brave and strong all the time. I'm your friend. From way back. You're not alone."

It was almost as if he had read her mind. But the problem was, Wynn had come to a different conclusion. He thought she would be satisfied with the part of him he had to offer. But she wasn't, she couldn't be. At the tender age of eighteen, the two of them had connected on a level so deep they had almost been a single person.

Laughing, crying, feeling, loving.

She missed that terribly. She *wanted* that again. But she wouldn't let him see how much his kindness hurt. Kindness where there had once been love was a hollow offering.

She didn't want his pity. To confess her love and not have it returned might be worse than being alone.

"I appreciate your concern," she said. "But I'm fine. Can we please go to bed now?"

Wynn scooped her into his arms and carried her to his room. They undressed each other without speaking.

Felicity had nothing left to say—or more to the point, nothing that wouldn't betray what she felt for him. Wynn didn't want her love.

That hurt more than anything that had transpired in the last month.

She ran her hands over his naked body, trying to memorize the feel of him for the long winter nights ahead. Nights when she would be flying somewhere far away. Nights when he would be in New York with his daughter.

When she curled her fingers around his sex, he shuddered. Closed his eyes. Groaned.

Felicity loved pleasuring him, but she wasn't special. Any woman could and would take her place.

Doggedly, she shoved those thoughts aside. She released him and climbed into bed. When he joined her, she sighed, feeling the pieces of her world settle into a harmonious whole. Words of love and pleading trembled on her tongue, choking her.

But she bit her lip, silencing the young, ridiculously naive girl who still lived inside her.

Wynn moved the hair from her face. He cupped her cheek, traced her collarbone, brushed lightly over each nipple in rapid succession.

It was too much and not enough. Need filled her, overwhelmed her.

When he rolled the condom on, she was shocked to feel pique…hurt. Did she really expect him to take chances? Surely not.

Tonight, she was content to lie back and receive him into her body. Emotional turmoil and exhaustion made this moment bittersweet.

How many times could she have sex with him and keep her secrets?

Perhaps Wynn picked up on her unusual passivity. How could he not? Where once they reveled in rough passion, tonight he offered her terrifying tenderness.

She didn't want that. She didn't. But when she tried to fight him and make him lose control, he defeated her.

The diabolical man gave her the most exquisite orgasm with his talented fingers, and then he thrust inside her while the tremors still rippled from her sex to her heart.

He was not as much in control as he pretended. He came hard, with a ragged moan, and slumped on top of her.

Felicity felt her heart shatter. She couldn't stay until January. How could she bear it?

Minutes passed. She didn't know how many.

When Wynn at last moved away from her, she sat up on the side of the bed with her back to him. "Good night," she whispered.

"Where are you going?"

When she glanced over her shoulder, his expression was both angry and befuddled.

"I need to be alone," she said. Scooping up her clothes, she walked out and shut the door.

Felicity felt a chill in the air after that night. She and Wynn slept in their own rooms. Their conversations became limited to pedestrian exchanges about Ayla. Wynn, for his part, did remember that she needed a dress.

He came home early on Tuesday and shooed her out of the apartment. "Go find something gorgeous," he said. "I want to make every man at the party jealous."

Her jaw dropped. "We're still going?"

"Yes." His eyes seemed to telegraph a message.

"But I thought we were cross with each other."

His lopsided smile acknowledged the cold war. "You're the one who changed, Fliss. I'm here whenever you want me. But I won't make love to a woman who's going through the motions. Not even if that beautiful and desirable woman is you."

Guilt choked her, confused her. What was he saying?

"I won't be gone long," she said.

"Take all the time you need."

By Thursday afternoon, Felicity was a bundle of nerves. She was going to a huge society party with a man who was equal parts handsome and dangerous. Wynn walked down the hall just as she came out of her room.

His eyes flared, and she could swear his jaw dropped. "Wow," he said.

"Is it too much?"

Her dress was red satin, sin red. Strapless except for two tiny rhinestone shoulder ribbons that were more for show than support. The gown nipped in at the waist. Ballet length. She had chosen silvery stiletto pumps that gave her additional height. A faux fur wrap protected her shoulders.

Wynn shook his head slowly. "Not too much at all. You look like a younger, hotter Jackie Kennedy. If she were a blonde."

Felicity grinned. "First of all, no one was hotter

than Jackie. And secondly, that's too many qualifiers for a real compliment."

He reached out an arm and pulled her close. "Then what if I settle for saying you look exquisite." He kissed her lazily, not even worrying about her lipstick. "This hair thing makes me want to bite your neck."

"It's called a French twist." *And I'm pretty sure you know that.* Sometimes he liked to play the clueless male when he was anything but...

"They called to say the babysitter is on her way up." His gaze remained on her lips as if he wasn't finished fooling around.

Felicity smoothed her skirt. Missy hadn't been available, but she had vouched for a friend who was in school at NYU. "I'll fix my lipstick and meet you at the door."

"Don't bother," he muttered. "I'll probably ruin it again."

The heat in his gaze told her he was serious.

She cupped his cheek in one hand, feeling the smooth, warm skin. He had clearly just shaved. "You're gorgeous in that tux, Mr. Oliver. Who would have ever believed the two of us would be going out on the town all glitzy and glamorous?"

His expression softened. "I didn't know enough back then to fantasize about a night like this. But now I do. Can we call a truce, Fliss?"

"Yes." She sighed. "I'm sorry I've been difficult."

"You're definitely worth the effort," he joked.

She punched his arm. "I'll see you in a minute."

* * *

Half an hour later they were in the car headed to their destination. Felicity sat with her hands in her lap, unwilling to give the driver anything to gossip about, even if the man was discreet. She wrapped her fingers around a small red satin clutch that held her lipstick and a few other necessities.

Wynn touched her arm. "You okay?"

"I'm great," she said.

This holiday season might be her best Christmas ever. Or the worst. That remained to be seen.

Suddenly, something occurred to her. She couldn't believe she hadn't thought of it before. She half turned to face him. "Where do you usually spend Christmas?" she asked. "Here? Or in Falcon's Notch?" Why would the man build such a fabulous house and not use it? Especially with a baby daughter. The time was ripe to build new traditions.

He shrugged. "Here, as a rule."

"And why did you build the house in Tennessee?"

"You want the truth?"

His answer surprised her. "I suppose," she said slowly.

His self-derisive grin was illuminated by the passing lights. "I wanted to prove a point. That I made something of myself. I hoped everybody in that small, gossipy town would see my extravagant house and maybe be sorry for all the times they sneered at me and my family."

"Oh, Wynn…" Her heart turned over in her chest.

His hands fisted on his knees. "It's not important," he said. "It's just an empty house."

She reached out and took one of his hands in hers. For once, his fingers were cold. "You have nothing to prove, Wynn. You made your point years ago. You used your brains and your drive to take you to the top. That's something to be proud of..."

They had been speaking in low voices. Low enough that the driver couldn't hear. Suddenly, the car pulled to the curb.

Wynn released her under the pretext of getting out. But she wondered if her words had bothered him.

The party was in full swing when they made it upstairs. Felicity was not at all shy, but the crush of people was a little disconcerting.

She clung to Wynn's hand as they made their way through the throng.

He knew everyone, it seemed. Men shook his hand. A few even hugged him. But it was the women Felicity noticed. And the way they looked at her with envy and chagrin.

How many eligible women were there in Manhattan? And how many of them had Wynn dated?

She wasn't sure she wanted to know.

They grabbed hors d'oeuvres and found a spot near one of the floor-to-ceiling windows. The view of the city at night was spectacular.

Wynn took her tiny purse and slid it into his pocket. "Do you want wine?" he asked.

She leaned into him. "Don't leave me," she whispered, joking. "I might never find you again."

"Whatever you say." He grinned at her. It was such a lighthearted, happy smile her heart jumped.

They ate in silence. The food was amazing. A well-known celebrity chef had provided the elegant smorgasbord.

Suddenly someone began clearing the space in front of the band who had been playing a wide range of upbeat music rich with rumbling bass. A dance floor appeared, and a murmur swept through the crowd.

The lead vocalist took the mike and waved a hand. "Grab your best guy or girl and let's get into the holiday spirit."

Wynn brushed the backs of his fingers over Felicity's hot cheek. The room was packed, and it was stuffy. "Shall we, Fliss?" His eyes were warm and mesmerizing.

"Sure." She knew it was a bad idea, but what else could she say? She yearned to dance with him.

Wynn got rid of their plates. They shared a glass of champagne, and then he held her hand and pulled her into the middle of the floor. In less time than it took to breathe his name, they were locked in each other's arms.

The music had changed. Now every pick was a slow song. Ed Sheeran, Adele, Olivia Rodrigo, Taylor Swift...even a little Tony Bennett. But the one that threatened to bring her to her knees was a Jason Mraz number. The chorus touched every vulnerable nerve inside her. *I'm yours.*

It was true. She belonged to Wynn in a way that couldn't be explained. He didn't own her. He didn't even want her forever.

None of that mattered. She was his.

She gave herself a mental shake. Now wasn't the moment to fret about the future. She would cherish this time with Wynn and make it count. When she wrapped her arms around his neck and rested her cheek against his shoulder, she heard a hitch in his breathing, felt his arms tighten.

They swayed to the music, oblivious to the other dancers. One song melted into the next. Wynn's presence surrounded her—his familiar touch, his hard, warm body, his masculine scent.

Because they were so close, she felt the evidence of his arousal pushing against her. Desire accelerated her heartbeat. She pressed her fingertips into the fabric of his jacket.

"I love you…" She breathed the words in a whisper, knowing he couldn't hear. Her chest hurt. How could he not feel it, too? He held her so tenderly. Didn't he believe they could find their way back to a love that was real? Or better yet, forge a new path?

Wynn Oliver and Felicity Vance made sense together. They were two parts of a whole. Cut from the same cloth, formed in the tiny mountain community that still influenced them both at some level.

His fingers caressed the nape of her neck. "Damn, I want you," he growled at her ear.

She pulled back and looked up at him. "How much longer do we need to stay?" She *wanted* things, too. Dancing with him like this was seductive and wonderful. Only once before had they come close to such an experience.

It had been spring of their senior year in high school.

Neither of them could afford prom tickets. Instead, Wynn had taken her out in the woods with a boom box and slow danced with her until they tumbled to the ground and found the connection they craved.

Now Wynn's cheekbones were ruddy with color. His eyes seemed not quite focused. His harsh breathing made his chest rise and fall. "I've seen everybody I need to see," he said hoarsely. His gaze cataloged her features.

"Two more songs?" she said. "And then we'll go?"

He kissed her long and hard, seemingly unconcerned they were in a crowd of people. At last, he pulled back from the kiss but didn't release her. "Two songs," he said, his eyes glittering.

She nodded slowly, seeing the frustration in his gaze but feeling the tenderness in his touch. He felt *something* for her. But was it enough to change his mind about love and relationships?

Felicity lost herself in the music. Her body hummed with arousal. Dancing with the all-grown-up Wynn was an erotic dream she hadn't known she craved. Halfway through the second song, she knew she couldn't wait. "Let's go," she said.

Wynn frowned. "Why?"

She searched his face, wishing he could read her mind. She wasn't brave enough to tell him the whole truth. She couldn't voice the real reason she was here. So she settled for the only truth he would accept. "Because I want you," she said. "Now."

Fifteen

Wynn's entire body went rigid. He might have been holding his breath. "Yes," he muttered.

Without further discussion, he took her by the hand and led her through the maze of people. The crowd's mood was celebratory. Alcohol flowed. The band finished the last slow song and kicked things up a notch.

No one paid a bit of attention to the tall man and the blonde woman winding their way toward the door.

When they finally reached the hallway, the reduction in decibels was striking. Wynn backed Felicity against the wall and kissed her until they were both trembling and panting.

"It's a long way to your apartment," she said. Her words weren't exactly a complaint, but the thought of waiting seemed impossible.

Hunger was a ravenous tempter, luring them both with soft growls and shivering delight.

Wynn looked around wildly. "I have an idea," he said. He tugged her onto the freight elevator and pushed a button.

The party was in full swing on the fourth floor of the warehouse, but two levels down—the floor where Wynn and Felicity now got off—the huge empty space was cavernous and dark. Their footsteps echoed eerily.

Felicity clutched his hand. "This is spooky."

His grin was a flash of white teeth in the gloom. "I swear I'll protect you, little girl."

She gave him a wry look. "Why does that sound like the big bad wolf coaxing me to my doom?"

Wynn stopped short, took her hand, and placed it palm flat on his chest—right over his thundering heartbeat. "If you're doomed, I'll be right there with you."

She felt the rhythm of his excitement. It echoed hers. "Is that supposed to make me feel better?" she teased.

When he released her, he cupped her face in his hands. "We're about to do something a little dangerous and chancy. If you'd rather call a cab, we can head home now."

She shivered hard, feeling the lure of Wynn's potent masculinity. "I'm not afraid," she said. "Not ever with you."

"Good." Deliberately, he cupped her breast and squeezed, thumbing the nipple through the fabric. His breathing was harsh, ragged.

In the near dark, his expression was hard to read. A man intent on sex had a certain focus, a recognizable posture. But this was more. Wynn seemed almost desperate.

He led her deeper into the uninhabited space. Nothing had been done here, no renovation, no upkeep. At some point, the walls had been ripped out...or maybe there were never walls to begin with.

They were now as far from the hallway and the elevator as possible. Though light streamed through huge windows, the deep shadows were perfect cover for clandestine activities.

Felicity caught the lapel of Wynn's jacket. "I'm nobody, but what happens if you get caught?"

"Not a damn thing, I swear. We're not doing anything wrong."

She exhaled. "Okay."

He backed her against a steel girder and put his hands under her skirt. "Hell, Fliss. Your skin is so soft."

The metal was cold against her back. He started at her knees and caressed his way up her thighs to her waist. His hands were large and slightly rough. As he toyed with her panties, he distracted her with a kiss. When he ripped the silky bikinis in half, she gaped at him.

"How am I going to get home?" she squeaked, feeling a blush suffuse her entire body.

Wynn's low chuckle made the hair on her arms stand up. "We'll have fun on the way, won't we?"

He didn't give her time to process that thought. Instead, he dove in for another kiss, this one harder and more demanding than the last. For a panicked moment she thought he was going to take down her hair.

She flinched and touched his hand when he removed a single pin. But then reason must have prevailed. "Sorry, baby," he said. "I know I have to keep you looking presentable."

"It might be a good idea." Her breath was ragged. "We still have to leave this building."

"True." He bit her neck, a quick sharp nip, just below her ear. "I could devour you," he said, the words husky and low. "I'm not sure I like how you make me feel."

Her anger flared. "I'm not seducing you, Wynn. If this isn't what you want, let's call this quits. We already know it's temporary."

He stepped back, visibly disconcerted. "How did I forget you have a temper? Of course, this is what I want, you silly woman. Why else would I be trying to snag a quickie in an old, deserted warehouse?"

She pouted. "A quickie? How disappointing…"

He choked out a laugh, put a hand to his forehead and stared up into the shadowy rafters. "I never do stupid things when I'm alone."

"Don't blame me." She reached out and unzipped his pants, then delved into his snug knit boxers to find the hard length of him. "At the risk of sounding shallow, I love your body. Especially *this* part." When she squeezed him, he shuddered and cursed.

He pushed her hand away. "I'm on a hair trigger, Fliss. No foreplay. Not tonight."

She caught his wrist and brought it to her mouth. Kissing the spot where his pulse pounded, she sank her teeth into the skin. "I'm not getting down on that nasty floor, Mr. Bigshot, not even for you."

"You underestimate me, darlin'." He scooped her up. "Put your arms around my neck."

A draft of icy air found its way to her bare ass. Her skirt was bunched so badly the wrinkles would be horrendous. But when Wynn kissed her again, all she could think about was how badly she wanted him inside her. She wrapped her legs around his waist and clung to him.

The kiss went on forever. Either they had both developed patience, or neither wanted this interlude to end.

She sucked his bottom lip into her mouth. "Tell me how hard you're going to do it."

He jerked back and stared at her. "Maybe I was going to be tender and gentle."

Her grin widened. "In a deserted warehouse on a cold December night? I don't think so. You're probably going to snap like a wild animal because you want me bad."

"Bad-*ly*," he taunted.

"Whatever..." She unknotted his tie. "Too bad this isn't a clip-on. I hope you know how to redo it." She tugged it free of his collar and dropped it on the floor. "Oh, but you're sophisticated now, aren't you, Wynn Oliver? You know all those fancy-man *GQ* skills."

"Brat. I paid a hundred and fifty bucks for that tie. It's Italian silk."

Now she started in on his shirt buttons. "What a ridiculous waste of money. Now, silk underpants, *that* would be another thing entirely. Think how the silk would caress your ba—"

He put his hand over her mouth. "Are we going to talk or screw?"

She cocked her head as she caressed his smooth chest. "Did you bring protection?"

"And if I said no?"

Her stomach fell. "Seriously?"

"I could pull out," he said. "When it's necessary."

"You would take that risk? With one baby in your life already?" She was shocked.

He rested his forehead against hers. "I'm teasing, Fliss. I have condoms. In my pocket."

"Oh. Well, that's good." She felt ridiculously embarrassed, given the circumstances.

He didn't even bother to conceal his amusement. His laughter echoed in the vaulted space. "No pregnancy scares, Fliss. I didn't think it would be so easy to lead you down that path."

"You're mean."

"You have no idea." He bent his head and caught her earlobe between his teeth. "I've needed you for hours. My dick is so hard it feels like stone. I may have a permanent injury."

She rubbed her thumbs over his cheekbones. "Poor baby. But you still haven't told me how you're going to do it. Tab A into slot B. Feel free to elaborate."

He went still, his hands under her thighs supporting her weight even as he pressed her against the beam.

He kissed her eyelids, one at a time. Then he found her mouth and ravaged it with gentle, thorough dominance.

When he could breathe, he stared at her. "I'm going in hard and deep, my Fliss. I'm gonna stretch you and fill you and make you forget your name. And when you come, I'll keep taking you harder and deeper still until you beg me to stop."

Her mouth fell open. "Oh."

"Oh, indeed." His smile was lopsided. When he moved slightly, a shaft of light highlighted his features—the straight noble nose, the sculpted lips. The broad forehead with the swath of dark hair she had rumpled. "I'll need your help. Try the right pocket. I don't want to drop you."

She twisted and reached, still clinging to his neck with one hand. "Got it," she said triumphantly.

"Now you'll have to put it on me."

Her eyes widened. "Um…"

"It's the only way, darlin'. Or else I'll have to set you down on the floor, and in case you haven't noticed, both of your shoes fell off."

She shuddered as she imagined her bare feet in all that dusty darkness. "Okay. I guess we can make it work."

"I'm going to let you down a little bit, but the beam will help. I won't drop you, I swear."

"This was a better idea when we were dancing."

He grinned. "I believe in us."

His joking, throwaway comment buried itself deep in her heart as a dagger of pain. He didn't. He really didn't.

"I'm ready," she said, ignoring the lingering hurt and concentrating on the immediate pleasure.

Carefully, he lowered her until she could reach his rigid sex. Quickly, she tore open the packet and extracted what she needed.

The cords on Wynn's neck stood out, either from the strain of the position or from excitement, or both.

She unrolled the latex over his smooth taut flesh, all the while resenting the need for protection. It was no effort at all to remember what it felt like to have him inside her with no barrier between them.

When the protection was in place, Wynn mumbled something inaudible. He had bent over at an angle that must be killing his back, but he didn't complain. "Grab my neck with both arms," he said.

"Got it." She did as he asked and marveled at his raw power when he lifted her higher on his body.

He nuzzled her nose with his as he took in a lungful of air. His skin was damp, his shirt askew. "Ready?"

She nodded, feeling something shift and burn in her chest. This was the beginning of heartbreak. She felt it, saw it, tried to run from it. But her own need for this man defeated her. "I'm ready," she whispered.

It took a moment. With both of them still mostly dressed, the logistics were tricky. But when Wynn found her entrance and surged deep, she cried out. The joy was incandescent. She loved feeling his body join hers.

He hadn't lied in his description. Even with the post for leverage, this position made her wholly dependent on his movements. He was in control. Completely.

"Am I hurting you?" he croaked.

"No." The single syllable was all she could manage. Already, her orgasm hovered, ready to suck her into the vortex. But she wanted more. She wanted everything.

His big hands clenched her ass, literally lifting her with brute strength. And when he brought her down hard on his sex, they both groaned.

Theoretically, it shouldn't have lasted more than a minute or two. They were both too close to the edge, and the physical demands of this coupling were intense for Wynn.

But he persisted.

"I like this," he muttered, his breath hot on her ear. "You're tight and perfect. I feel like the top of my head may explode when I come."

"Sounds painful."

He kissed her hard. His tongue dueled with hers, stealing her breath. "You have a smart mouth and a delectable ass. It's a lethal combo."

She wriggled in his arms, trying to get closer. "And you have the best, most wicked ideas. I never in a million years would have imagined Wynn Oliver having raunchy warehouse sex. But I love it."

"I can't get enough of you, Fliss."

She sensed he hadn't meant to say those words. They made him vulnerable. Or maybe not. Felicity had never been one to use sex as a weapon. "Take everything you want, Wynn." She kissed him slowly, tracing his lower lip with the tip of her tongue.

Without warning, he pulled her tightly into his embrace, grinding the base of his sex against her needy spot. She literally saw stars. Or flashes of light. Later, she couldn't re-create the precise memory of that moment no matter how hard she tried.

The climax was intense, and it went on forever.

She was still feeling the ripples when Wynn shouted her name and pounded into her. The hard metal post was the only point of solidarity when her world spiraled into madness.

To his credit, he never dropped her. Even when he lost his mind. He could barely breathe, but his hands and arms still supported her weight.

"Wow." She rested her cheek against his bare chest. "How rich are you?" she asked.

She felt the chuckle that rumbled through his chest at her non sequitur. "Why do you ask, my sweet?"

"I just wondered if you could afford to buy this warehouse. It's starting to grow on me."

Wynn buried his face in the curve of her neck, still trying to catch his breath. "I agree. But we both have very comfy beds back at my place, and I told the sitter we wouldn't be too late."

Felicity sighed. "I know." Suddenly, it occurred to her that her feet were still bare. "How are we going to pick up my shoes?"

He nuzzled the sensitive spot just below her ear. "There's a folding chair behind you. How bad could it be? I'll sit you down and bring you your sexy shoes."

"Ugh…" The chair was probably like everything else—coated in dust. But it wouldn't be as bad as stepping barefoot on the floor. "Okay," she said.

Wynn walked over to the one item of furniture they could see. Carefully, he put her in the seat and stepped back. "Hang on."

Moments later, he was back with her stilettos and something else.

"What's that?" she asked, pointing at his left hand.

His grin was rueful. "Your undies? I didn't think we should leave any evidence."

She hid a smile, giving him her most solemn nod of agreement. "Very wise, Mr. Oliver."

He stuffed her underwear in his pocket and squatted to put her shoes on her feet one at a time. With both his hands on her calf, she felt a simmer of longing. What would happen back at the apartment? Were they done for the night? Or was this only a beginning?

At last, he took her hand and helped her stand.

Felicity did her best to smooth her skirt. Maybe no one would look too closely.

Wynn handed her the clutch purse he'd been keeping in his pocket. "You might want to do a few repairs before we head back downstairs. You're a little *rumpled*."

"Thanks," she said wryly. When she opened her compact and took a peek, she winced. Her long-wear lip stain had reached its limit. Her French twist was still intact, but little tendrils of hair floated around her face. And the smudge-proof mascara was…well, smudged.

Quickly, she dealt with the problems. "Okay," she said. "That's the best I can do."

This time, Wynn didn't smile. He stared at her in

the semidarkness, his expression oddly blank. "You look beautiful, Fliss. Let's go. I've already called my driver."

Neither of them spoke in the elevator. But it was a short trip. In the lobby—also renovated—Wynn retrieved Felicity's wrap and tucked it around her shoulders.

When they stepped outside, she caught her breath. The air was sharp, and the wind cut deep. Wynn helped her into the car and scooted in behind her, slamming the door to keep the cold at bay.

As they rode down one street and then another, he pulled her against his side and warmed her hands in his.

It was far too late in the evening to put up a fight. She laid her head on his shoulder and watched dreamily as the lights flashed past the car window in a dizzying array.

Wynn was silent, his thoughts a mystery. Again, she wondered what would happen if she made the first move and expressed her feelings? His lovemaking was focused and overwhelming. He was often both tender and dominant in the way he touched her. Was it possible he felt something for her but was afraid to let down his guard? How could she break through that invisible barrier?

Sixteen

At the apartment, Wynn dealt with the babysitter while Felicity kicked off her uncomfortable high heels and curled up in front of the fire. The days of December were ticking by. She wondered if Wynn would hire someone to *deck the halls* for the holidays.

He had been a single man enjoying life in the big city. Presumably, he didn't spend many nights alone. This lovely apartment hadn't so much as a sprig of mistletoe to mark the season.

Maybe the lack of traditional decorations didn't bother him.

When he finally entered the room, he was yawning. "You didn't have to wait up for me," he said.

Suddenly, she felt it again. The awkwardness. The

uncertainty. "Well," she said, "I was still hyped from the party."

He cocked his head. "The party?"

She flushed. "You know what I mean."

"We haven't been spending the nights together, Fliss. I don't want to presume."

Her mind raced. Should she sleep with him? Or should she continue the process of pulling away? If she did it gradually, he might not guess how she felt.

But she was weak and selfish. She wanted what she wanted. *Who* she wanted. She wanted Wynn.

Before she could say another word, Wynn crossed the room and opened a drawer in the small escritoire. "Before you give me an answer, I should tell you I did something you may not like."

She tensed. "Oh?"

He turned around, holding a sheet of paper. "I had someone on my staff research your mother's personal info. Here's her address and phone number. I thought you might want to call her at some point."

Felicity felt her blood congeal. "You've wasted your time, Wynn. She lives with my uncle, and I *know* his address."

He stared at her. "Then use the phone number."

She stood, her bare toes curling against the carpet. She was ice-cold now, despite the fire. "Why?"

For the first time, she saw his frustration. "With your father gone, you're alone in the world, Fliss. I know that feeling, and it sucks."

Alone in the world? Her stomach curled in a knot. *What about you and Ayla?* She was certain he didn't mean his comments to sound dismissive or cruel, but she felt as if he had slapped her.

"That woman means nothing to me," she said. It was a lie. Even as she voiced the words, Felicity knew they weren't true. She *wanted* to be indifferent to Iris Vance, but that wasn't so easy.

Wynn scowled. "She's your mother, your flesh and blood."

Felicity took the paper, folded it and tossed it on the sofa with her purse. "Fine. I have her phone number. Are you happy?"

This standoff was especially upsetting after everything that had transpired between them earlier in the evening. They had gone from a romantic party and a scandalous rendezvous to the cold, harsh realities of life.

Wynn rubbed the center of his forehead. "I don't want to fight with you, but I have to go out of town in the morning, and I want you to be thinking about your mother and Christmas."

Several things hit her at once. "You're leaving?" She hated the hollow feeling in her belly.

He nodded. "I have to fly to LA for a meeting."

"In the middle of December?"

"It was scheduled for earlier, but Shandy's death rearranged things. I'll be back midweek. We can talk about Christmas then."

She lifted her chin. "What is there to talk about?"

"You mentioned celebrating in Falcon's Notch. That's not a bad idea. We could invite your mother and uncle to join us. New York might make them uncomfortable but being back in Tennessee should be okay."

Felicity was incredulous. "No, Wynn. Just no. I don't want to see Iris Vance *or* my uncle. Do you think I can just ignore a lie that was perpetrated for almost my entire life? No. I won't do it."

She hated the way he looked at her. As if she was being hysterical and unreasonable.

"It's late," he said. "Let's go to bed. Things will look better in the morning. They always do."

She crossed her arms and tried not to cry. "That's not really true. Sometimes they get worse. Besides, you're leaving."

He crossed the room and put his hands on her upper arms. "I won't be gone long." He kissed her thoroughly. "I'll miss you."

It would be so easy to melt into his embrace, to join him in his big, hedonistic bed with the soft sheets and the scent of him on the pillows. But that would only make her situation worse.

She steeled her resolve. "I had fun tonight. Thank you for taking me to the party. But I'm very tired, and I think I'll sleep better alone."

Flashing green eyes bored into hers. His jaw tightened. "Are you angry with me?"

She shook her head slowly, side to side. "Well, I'm not *happy.* Take your trip, Wynn. We'll talk when you get back."

"And you'll think about Christmas? You'll call your mother?"

The idea horrified her. "Sure," she lied. "If it will make you feel better."

"Good. You won't regret it."

Arrogant, infuriating man. How would he know?

"Safe travels," she said, picking up her things and heading for the door. "I'll set my alarm for seven. Is that early enough?"

"Yes. The car is coming at eight." He turned off the lights and followed her down the hallway to the door of her room. "We'll figure it out, Fliss. Don't be upset."

She saw the concern on his face and almost shouted at him. She didn't crave his compassion. She wanted his love.

"Good night," she said. Then she slipped into her room and locked the door.

The first day Wynn was gone dragged on forever. Ayla was her usual sunny self, but Felicity heard the echoing silence in the apartment and grieved. Wynn had a large personality. She felt his absence keenly.

On the second day, the sun shone from a blue sky. The thought of driving around the city amidst December traffic made her shudder. So she called Wynn's driver and made arrangements for him to act as chauffeur.

The older man was kind and had a dry sense of humor. He seemed happy to take them from store to store while Felicity knocked out her Christmas shopping. Six of her Knoxville-based friends would get packages in the mail with expensive designer scarves. For Ayla, Felicity picked out a soft, French-made baby doll with lifelike features. She also found a tiny red wool coat with a black velvet collar that was too cute to resist.

What to get Wynn was a puzzle. They were friends…
and lovers. But the man could buy anything he wanted.
In the end, she found the perfect gift in a small, exclusive gallery. It was an oil painting of the Smoky Mountains done in shades of blue and gray and mauve. The
picture had a mystical, haunting feel. Despite its beauty,
looking at the image made her achingly sad.

She and Wynn shared this heritage, but little else.
He had shut himself off from the intimacy of a long-
term relationship. Nothing she could do or say would
change his mind.

The third day Wynn was gone, Felicity got a text
from a colleague. Derek was a senior flight attendant
based in Dallas. He had a twenty-four-hour layover in
New York and wanted to see her. Big news to share.

The balmy weather had continued, so Felicity suggested meeting in Central Park and walking while
they talked.

She bundled Ayla in layers and pulled the fancy
stroller out of the closet. By now, she knew the im-
portance of a well-packed baby bag. In addition to
diapers and wipes and extra clothes, she added a se-
lection of lunch foods Ayla would like. Then she put
on nice jeans, a thin cashmere sweater and sneakers.

When she met Derek by the model boat pond, he
gave her a broad smile and wrapped her in a hug. "You
look amazing, Felicity. And a baby? I had no idea."

"She's not mine. It's a long story."

As they walked, she shared the highlights of her unexpected encounter with Wynn at Shandy's funeral…

skipping the private bits, of course. Derek listened with interest and asked a million questions.

The conversation was therapeutic.

The afternoon was low-drama and oddly comforting. Ayla cooed and waved at strangers. She loved stroller outings. In the park, there were endless entertainments for a curious little one.

After Felicity and Derek ate hot dogs on a park bench, she chuckled and wiped mustard off her fingers. "Enough about me," she said. "You're dragging out the suspense. I'm dying to know. What's your big news? I can't imagine you're leaving the airline. So what is it?"

He beamed. "I'm engaged."

"Seriously?" Derek had played the field for years. A very *big* field.

He nodded, his expression happy enough to make her jealous of his good fortune. "We met in London. Her name is Naomi. She's a physician's assistant at a local clinic. I had a bad allergy attack early in September when I was over there. Naomi nursed me back to health."

"Wow," she said, laughing. "It's like a movie."

"I know," he said, his expression smug.

"I'm so glad you texted me. This is awesome. Have you set a wedding date?"

"We're thinking late spring...and a honeymoon in Greece. I'd love for you to meet her."

Felicity hedged. "It would be hard for me to get away anytime soon because of the baby, but let's stay in touch."

Ayla had been napping contentedly in the stroller. Felicity knew it was time to get back.

"I'll walk with you," Derek said. "My hotel is in that direction."

When they were in front of Wynn's building, Derek raised an eyebrow. "This must be a pricey address."

Felicity nodded. "Wynn has done very well for himself, especially considering where we both started out in life."

Derek stared at her. "Wait a minute. Are you telling me this is the guy who broke your heart in high school? And you're *working* for him now?"

She winced. "I'm doing him a favor. It's complicated."

He glanced at his watch. "Damn. I have to go. But I want to hear the rest of this story, Felicity."

"No story," she said lightly. "Nothing to tell."

He kissed her on the mouth and wrapped her in a huge hug. Felicity didn't mind his boisterous affection. That was Derek's way.

She returned the kiss, but on the cheek, and hugged him back. "Take care of yourself," she said.

He squatted in front of the stroller. "Bye, little cutie."

From behind them, a deep voice with a chilly edge spoke. "Am I interrupting?"

Felicity spun around, her heart in her throat. "Wynn. You're back?"

He stared at her, his gaze narrowed. "I am. And who might this be? I see my daughter already knows him."

Hastily, Felicity made the introductions.

Derek shook Wynn's hand. "Nice to meet you, Mr.

Oliver. I hate to run, but I have a flight to catch." He smiled at Felicity. "I'll keep you posted."

When he loped off down the street, Wynn bent and took Ayla out of the stroller. "You girls have had a busy day."

She couldn't place the odd note in his voice. "Derek had a short layover. We were catching up." She felt guilty for no good reason, and that made her confused and defensive. "How was *your* flight?" she asked.

"Uneventful."

"And your meetings?"

"The same…"

Upstairs, he peeled Ayla out of her outerwear. Felicity took off her own coat and boots and began unloading the deep compartment on the back of the stroller. "I had planned on ordering a small pizza," she said, "but if you'd like something more substantial, we can get Chinese. Or whatever you want."

She followed Wynn as he took the baby into the living room and set her in front of her pile of toys.

He straightened and stared at her. "Is Derek in the running for happily-ever-after?" The words had sharp edges.

"Derek is a friend. I've known him forever."

"I'm sure you have," he said quietly. "You even told me so. When I asked if you had someone in mind to marry and have babies with, you said there were *plenty* of choices. And you mentioned *colleagues*, in particular."

She shivered with nerves. "Derek recently got engaged. He wanted to tell me in person." She was losing Wynn bit by bit. She could sense it. So it was now or never.

Inhaling sharply, she gazed at him, willing him to listen. Her pride didn't matter anymore. "Derek has always been just a friend to me. But I love *you*, Wynn."

His face went blank. Then he paled. "Don't say that."

"I have to. It's true."

"It's the holidays making you sentimental."

"Don't be ridiculous. I'm in love with you. Maybe at some level I never *stopped* loving you. But it's different this time. I'm not a kid anymore."

"We're good in bed. That's not love."

His words hurt her badly. "You can't tell me what I feel. I *love* you. At one time, you loved me, too. I'm begging you to give us another chance."

"No," he said, his tone curt.

She saw no softness in him anywhere. "What are you afraid of, Wynn?"

His eyes were blank. "Nothing. I've spent years learning how to survive and thrive on my own. It's all I know now. And I like it that way. I can't be the man in your little fantasy. That's not me."

Tears stung her eyes. "But when you make love to me, it feels so real."

His jaw tightened. "Women are good at deceiving themselves." He lifted one shoulder and let it fall… a fatalistic shrug. "You told me you wanted to leave New York. So go. I think that will be best for both of us at this point."

"But who will look after Ayla?"

"I'll find someone." His features were carved in stone, remote…unforgiving.

"You told me I'm the only person you trust to care for her."

"Well, I was wrong, then, wasn't I? There will be others." The stoic expression in his green eyes scored her soul. "Did you call your mother?"

"No." She wanted to say it wasn't any of his business, but things were bad enough without provoking him.

His jaw tightened. "Even though you told me you would?" He glanced down at the floor where Ayla played and then back at Felicity. His expression turned bleak. "Just go, Felicity. Put us out of our misery. If there are no flights this evening, you can grab a room near the airport. I'll ship whatever you can't take with you."

Felicity didn't know what to say or do. The situation had imploded so rapidly and drastically she was in shock. "I think you're overreacting," she said quietly. "You're giving up on us, and I don't know why."

It was a last-ditch effort to reach him.

His terse smile was no smile at all. "There is no *us*, Felicity. I told you that all along. We've had fun in bed, but we're done. Pack your bags. Go back to your old life. You told me from the very beginning that's what you wanted to do. Nothing has changed."

Twelve hours later, Felicity sat at her boarding gate, numb and filled with despair. The winter morning sky was gray and sullen. A weather front during the night had returned the city's weather to seasonal December temps.

She should never have gone to Shandy's funeral. Should never have agreed to Wynn's plan.

If she hadn't entangled her life with his, she would still have her work routines, her friends, her sense of normalcy. And a heart that was whole.

She didn't know what to do.

Wynn fed the baby strained peaches and tried to smile. His daughter. His precious daughter. But even as he interacted with the little girl, there was a gaping hole where his heart had been.

Now, twice in his life he had made an unforgivable mistake. The first one when he left Felicity and Falcon's Notch behind as a teenager. The second yesterday when he allowed his own fears to consume and control him. When he treated the woman he loved with cold derision.

Had he really thought he could send her away without damaging his own soul?

He loved Felicity Vance. Deeply, irrevocably. Perhaps he had always loved her. Why else would he have concocted a plan to keep her under his roof? Why else would he have made love to her with such desperation and passion?

He stared blankly at the small TV on the kitchen counter. Before Ayla came into his life, he would have been toggling between morning news programs, listening to every breaking story.

Now, the TV was on mute. But the graphic at the bottom of the screen caught his eye. *Knoxville-bound jet skids off icy runway at LaGuardia.*

Nausea rose in his throat.

Felicity lived in Knoxville. And he had sent her to the airport.

As panic fluttered in his chest, he ran the odds in his head. She might have flown out last night. Or maybe she had left via JFK or Newark.

But her airline operated multiple routes out of La-Guardia.

The muted newscaster, her hair perfectly styled, looked straight into the camera with a serious expression. Her lips formed the words printed on the screen. *Possible casualties.*

Wynn grabbed his phone. Started jabbing in numbers.

Though he pulled every string he could, it took him an hour—a whole damn hour—to get Ayla's care covered. To make the terrifying discovery that Felicity's name was indeed on the passenger manifest. To make the frustrating trip from Manhattan to the airport. To get as close to the runways as possible.

Every variety of law enforcement official swarmed the area. In addition to the usual security precautions, yellow tape cordoned off a wide swath of real estate.

An NYPD officer waved him off. "Sorry, sir. No civilian admittance. Check the airport's website. They have a phone number to call for information."

Wynn shook with helpless rage. Not at the man doing his job, but at his own culpability.

Fliss was out in that accident somewhere. He was going to do whatever it took to reach her.

Fortunately, it occurred to his terror-addled brain

that he had friends in high places. FAA buddies. The first one he called answered. Twenty minutes later, Wynn had the credentials he needed to metaphorically jump the fence.

The runway was a nightmare. Emergency vehicles everywhere. All incoming flights were being diverted. He didn't know or care where or why. His entire focus was on the crippled plane sitting drunkenly with one wingtip in the water.

Red and blue flashing lights made it hard to see. He jogged doggedly in the direction of the accident. It was a smallish jet. Probably a two-by-two configuration. How many people would have been on board?

Smoke billowed from one engine. The safety slides had deployed.

Where was Felicity in this chaotic nightmare?

And then it dawned on him. All he had to do was text her.

No answer. Damn.

Now he was close enough to smell jet fuel. The FDNY guys and gals were spraying foam from stem to stern.

EMT vehicles had parked wherever they could find space. Patients were being treated on the spot.

Wynn's desperation increased. How was he going to find her?

Seventeen

When Wynn glanced at his watch, he saw that forty-five minutes had passed since he'd made it into the restricted area.

Fliss was alone in this mess. And he had told her there was nothing between them but sex. His heart clenched. Where was she?

Finally…at last, he spotted her. Sitting on the bare ground. Wrapped in a silver emergency blanket, her head bowed.

He approached her cautiously, crouched in front of her. "Fliss." He said her name quietly.

She didn't look up.

"Fliss." He touched her knee this time. She was wearing black pants, ankle boots and a pink turtleneck.

But no coat. "Fliss. It's me. Wynn. Talk to me, honey. You're okay. I'm not going to leave you."

She lifted her head, her eyes glassy with shock. Her lips were blue. A tiny smudge of blood on her cheek worried him. "I don't have my stuff," she said, sounding confused. "They wouldn't let us take our carry-ons or purses." Tears welled in her eyes. "I don't have my driver's license or my credit cards. I don't have *anything*," she whispered.

Wynn took her face in his hands. Seeing her wet cheeks and drenched blue eyes killed him. "That's not true," he said gruffly. "You have me." Every cold, brutal word he had thrown at her came back to haunt him, making his throat raw and speech damn near impossible.

He rose to his feet and addressed a nearby female EMT. "Ma'am. Has this lady been checked out?"

"Yes, sir. No injuries. But shock, of course."

"May I take her now?"

A uniformed police officer joined the medic. The man frowned at Wynn. "In about half an hour we'll start loading the passengers on a bus to drive them to the terminal."

"Not this one." Wynn stared the man down. He wasn't leaving without Felicity.

"How did you even get out here?" the officer asked.

Wynn pulled out his phone and showed his credentials. "She's cold and miserable. I'm happy to give you every bit of my personal contact information, but I'm taking her home."

The cop looked at Felicity. "Do you want to go with this man, ma'am?"

Felicity peered up at the officer from her seat on the ground. She studied his face, and then she turned to look at Wynn.

A sick feeling flooded his veins. What was he going to do if she put up a fight? He couldn't kidnap her.

After what seemed like forever, she spoke. "Yes," she said. "I'd like to go home."

It was a helluva long way from the runway to where Wynn had parked his car. Felicity was in no shape to walk that distance.

He helped her to her feet. "I'm going to carry you," he said, making his words matter-of-fact and calm.

She stared at him for the longest time. "No," she said simply. "I'll walk."

Before he could say a word, she turned and began trudging toward the distant terminal, the silver blanket dragging behind her.

Wynn cursed helplessly. "You can't," he said. He grabbed her arm, halting her progress. "You were just involved in an airplane crash. The shock is impairing your judgment." He took the emergency wrap from her, removed his heavy coat and put it around her shoulders. Then he bent to scoop her into his arms.

But she eluded him. For the first time, he saw the cloudy confusion in her eyes go clear for a moment. Her gaze judged him and found him wanting. "I'm going to walk."

By the time they made it to Wynn's car, Felicity was

stumbling, but she refused to let him touch her, not even to hold her elbow.

He opened the passenger door, she got in, and he ran around to the driver's side. When they merged into the constant flow of airport traffic, Felicity twisted her hands in her lap. "I need to borrow a credit card, please," she said, "until I can take care of my accounts." Her voice was flat. "And please drop me at the Wellstar Hotel. It's the cheapest, closest place to stay."

Wynn reined in his temper. "Don't be absurd. You're coming home with me."

They were stopped at a light. Felicity jerked open the car door. "No, thank you," she said. And then she was gone, swallowed up in a crowd of people crossing the intersection.

Wynn stared, incredulous. The light changed. A symphony of car horns blared behind him. He eased forward, trying to keep Felicity in sight. His blood pressure shot up.

There wasn't a parking spot in ten city blocks. So he ran up onto the curb in front of a small floral business and shoved the gearshift into Park. He jumped out and ran after her, yelling. "Stop, Fliss. You're acting crazy."

A middle-aged Hispanic shopkeeper glared at him. "Don't you call a woman *loca, mi hijo*. It's rude."

Wynn gave the lady a tight smile as he ran by but didn't answer. He was worried sick about Felicity. What if she had a concussion?

He caught her in the next block. "You can have my credit card," he said, panting. "But let me take you to the hotel and check you in."

She was weaving on her feet, her pallor alarming. "Okay."

When they got back to his car, a cop was writing a ticket and tucking it under the windshield wiper. The man frowned. "Good thing you showed up. I was about to call a tow truck."

Wynn gritted his teeth. "Sorry, officer. This lady was in the crash at LaGuardia. I'm trying to get her to the doctor."

The policeman's expression was dubious. He looked at Felicity. "Do you need any help, ma'am?"

Felicity thought about it. For one panicked second, Wynn thought she was going to let the NYPD take care of her.

"No," she finally said. "But thank you."

Wynn folded the ticket and put it in his pocket. Felicity was worth it.

Because he was afraid of what she might do next, he drove her to the hotel as she had asked. Once they had a room, he called his personal physician and requested a house call.

There were times when he wasn't at all squeamish about throwing his money around. This was one of them.

Felicity didn't want to see a doctor, but he didn't give her a choice. Standing in the hallway during the exam felt like an eternity. When the middle-aged physician exited, he gave Wynn a wry smile.

"I like your lady," he said. "She'll be fine, but I've left a light sedative. She may have nightmares, you know."

"Thank you," Wynn said. "I really appreciate it."

When the man waved and entered the elevator, Wynn knocked quietly on Felicity's door and stepped inside. She was sitting on the side of the bed looking lost.

He didn't know what to do. His heart was cracking in half, and it hurt like hell.

He had messed up so badly, he wasn't sure if anything could be fixed. Maybe it was too late.

"Fliss. The doc says you're going to be okay. But he wants you to take the meds so you can rest tonight."

She turned her head in his direction, her gaze dull. "It's hours till bedtime. I won't forget."

"Honey..." He knelt on the floor beside the bed and took her hand. "I didn't mean those things I said yesterday. I was scared, scared that I could never be the man you deserve. I couldn't bear the thought of us trying another relationship and me screwing it up. I acted like a lunatic. God knows, I don't deserve it, but please forgive me."

"You don't love me."

The pain in her eyes crucified him. He swallowed hard. "Yes. Yes, I do. Enough for ten lifetimes, but I thought it was better to let you find somebody else. A guy less selfish than me. Less driven. Less cold."

She shrugged. "You're making excuses. But it doesn't really matter, does it? We were never going to be anything more than what we've been for the last month. Temporary lovers. And now, not even that."

"Fliss, I—"

She interrupted him. "Who has the baby?"

"My admin. Missy's mother. I called her as soon as I heard about the accident."

She pulled her hand from his grasp and wrapped her arms around her waist. "You should get back to your daughter. It was kind of you to check on me, but I'm fine."

She was so clearly *not* fine.

He bowed his head, wondering how to reach her... or even if he could.

"Felicity," he said quietly. "I love you."

When she flinched, he hit bottom.

"Don't," she said, her voice husky. "Don't you dare say those words."

"It's true." He shook his head slowly. "I didn't even realize it until you were gone. How stupid can a man be? I guess I was in deep denial. I was panicked, Fliss. Terrified that you would walk away. In fact, you'd already told me you *wanted* to leave. It was easier to pretend I didn't care than to imagine my life without you again."

"Lust," she said. "You felt lust."

"Yes. But so much more than that. You brought joy to my life, Fliss. And meaning."

She shook her head. "Your daughter did that. She's the only person you're interested in loving forever. I'm not on the list. You made that very clear."

His eyes burned. "God, Fliss, when I saw that news story, my heart stopped. I've never been so scared in my life."

"You're absolved of any and all guilt." She waved a hand. "Please go. I'd like to rest now."

"Let me stay," he croaked. "Let me hold you. That's all. I need to know you're alive. Maybe in about a hundred years I'll be able to forget about seeing that plane half in the water…and the smoke…" He trailed off, feeling sick.

Felicity stood and walked to the window. "You didn't cause the accident, Wynn. It was nothing but a coincidence. I'm fine. You're letting guilt make you say things you don't mean."

He jumped to his feet and crossed the room. "I love you," he shouted. "Why can't you believe me?"

Her gaze was tragic, her posture as fragile as a spun glass figurine. "You feel sorry for me. That's different."

He struggled to speak past the knot in his throat. "I love you. I loved you as a stupid teenage boy, and now I love you as a man loves a woman. You're mine, Fliss. Even if you walk away, you'll still be mine. I adore you."

She started to shake, and tears rained down her face. She was so pale, he thought she might faint. "No," she whispered.

"Please sit down, honey. Please."

This time when he took her arm, she didn't fight him. But she stopped in the center of the room and faced him. "Don't say it if it's not true. I couldn't bear it, Wynn."

He cupped her face in his hands and kissed her softly on the lips. "I love you, Felicity Vance. For better or for worse. It's true. I'm so sorry I hurt you."

She collapsed into his arms as if the sheer will that

had kept her going for hours evaporated. They clung to each other. He stroked her hair.

"I love you, Felicity," he said. "I'll keep saying it for as long as it takes."

"Okay."

A rueful smile tipped up the corners of his mouth. "Okay?"

"I love you, too," she sighed.

He shuddered hard, feeling a tsunami of relief. Scooping her into his arms, he carried her to the bed. "A short nap," he said. "And then I'll take you home."

When he laid her on the mattress and came down beside her, she touched his cheek. "Years ago, you swore you would never propose to me again, So I'll be the one to ask. Will you marry me, Wynn? May I adopt Ayla with you?"

He couldn't speak at all. He nodded, burying his face against her breast.

Felicity stroked his hair. "We'll be okay this time. Won't we?"

He hugged her tightly, feeling the curves of the woman who had seduced him with every fiber of her being, body and soul. "We're going to be incredible, Felicity Vance. Just you wait and see."

December 25

Wynn cuddled his daughter, who wore a green velvet dress with an appliquéd reindeer, as he watched his brand-new wife from across the room. A week ago, he and Felicity had married each other in a small, intimate New York chapel. Ayla's adoption would not be final for some time, but it was in the works.

On the twenty-third, the three of them had come home to the house in Falcon's Notch to spend the holidays. Wynn hadn't pushed, but Felicity had decided on her own to invite her mother and uncle for a short visit. They had arrived this afternoon.

The Christmas evening meal had been simple, but that was for the best under the circumstances. Felicity's family seemed in awe of his home and not entirely comfortable, though he had tried his best to make them so.

Wynn and Felicity had exchanged gifts last night by the fire. Unfortunately, there had been no time to get a tree. Next year, he promised himself.

The beautiful painting of the Smokies Felicity had given him would hang in his home office. Wynn wanted it in his study where he could see it often and remember the lessons he had learned from the mountains.

To Felicity, he had given a diamond solitaire necklace, one that matched her engagement ring. Before they were married, she had protested that she didn't need a ring, but he had been adamant.

Now, seeing it and the wedding band on her finger gave him a deep sense of pride and peace. She was his and he was hers.

Felicity rose and came to where he stood, smiling at him in a way that made his heart jerk in his chest. Iris and Felicity's uncle were leaving in the morning. Wynn would have the rest of the week and the beginning of the New Year to make love to his new wife and to create a romantic holiday week they would always remember.

He touched her cheek. "Do they like the surprise?" Felicity's uncle was a huge baseball fan. Apparently, so was Iris. Wynn and Felicity had given them a set of tickets to spring training and a premium room at a fancy hotel for a week and a half.

Felicity smiled. "They're thrilled. But I think they feel bad they don't have something for us. I tried to tell them their visit was gift enough."

He searched her face. "And you're sure you're okay with all this?"

"Not entirely, but I'm working on it. I have so much happiness and love bursting out of me right now, it would be petty not to share it."

He pulled her close and laughed when Ayla predictably went for a lock of Felicity's hair. "I love you, Mrs. Oliver," he said. "No more running away for either of us."

Felicity rested her cheek over his heart and sighed. "I know Ayla is ours, but I'd like to have at least one more."

Shocked, he pulled back to see her face more clearly. "You're not..."

She laughed. "Pregnant? No. Not yet. But I'd like to try."

His hand trembled as he smoothed her hair from her face. "Yes. Me, too. But not too soon. I need some time to spoil my new wife."

"That goes both ways, Wynn. You're not alone anymore. Ayla and I are going to drive you nuts with hugs and kisses, aren't we, little one?"

The baby blew bubbles, seeming to indicate her agreement.

Wynn stared over Felicity's head and out the plate glass window that framed a dramatic section of the Smokies' highest peaks.

He had come full circle in this place that had held both pain and pleasure. He and Felicity would never forget their past, both the good and the bad. But from now on, they would build on the love that had survived all these years.

This was his best Christmas ever, and it was only the beginning...

* * * * *

Look for more novels from
USA TODAY *bestselling author Janice Maynard*
and Harlequin Desire!

The Men of Stone River series
After Hours Seduction
Upstairs Downstairs Temptation
Secrets of a Playboy

WE HOPE YOU ENJOYED
THIS BOOK FROM

H HARLEQUIN
DESIRE

*Luxury, scandal, desire—welcome to
the lives of the American elite.*

Be transported to the worlds of oil barons, family dynasties,
moguls and celebrities. Get ready for juicy plot twists,
delicious sensuality and intriguing scandal.

6 NEW BOOKS AVAILABLE EVERY MONTH!

#2905 THE OUTLAW'S CLAIM

Westmoreland Legacy: The Outlaws • by Brenda Jackson

Rancher Maverick Outlaw and Sapphire Bordella are friends with occasional benefits. But when Phire must marry at her father's urging, their relationship ends...until they learn she's carrying Maverick's baby. Now he'll stop at nothing to stake his claim...

#2906 CINDERELLA MASQUERADE

Texas Cattleman's Club: Ranchers and Rivals • by LaQuette

Ready to break out of her shell, Dr. Zanai James agrees to go all out for the town's masquerade ball and meets handsome rancher Jayden Lattimore. Their attraction is instantaneous, but can their connection survive meddling families bent on keeping them apart?

#2907 MARRIED BY MIDNIGHT

Dynasties: Tech Tycoons • by Shannon McKenna

Ronnie Moss is in trouble. The brilliant television host needs a last-minute husband to fulfill her family's marriage mandate before she turns thirty—at midnight. Then comes sexy stranger Wes Brody, who volunteers himself. But is this convenient arrangement too good to be true?

#2908 SNOWED IN SECRETS

Angel's Share • by Jules Bennett

After distillery owner Sara Hawthorne and Ian Ford spend one hot night together, they don't expect to see each other again...until he shows up for their scheduled interview about her family business. Now snowed in, can they keep it professional?

#2909 WHAT HAPPENS AFTER HOURS

404 Sound • by Kianna Alexander

Recording studio exec Miles Woodson needs a showstopping act for his charity talent show, and R & B superstar Cambria Harding fits the bill. But when long days working together become steamy nights, can these opposites make both their passion project and relationship work?

#2910 BAD BOY WITH BENEFITS

The Kane Heirs • by Cynthia St. Aubin

Sent to audit his distillery, Marlowe Kane should keep her distance from bad boy owner Law Renaud. But when a storm prevents her from getting home, they can't resist, and their relationship awakens a passion in both that could cost them everything...

SPECIAL EXCERPT FROM

(H) HARLEQUIN

DESIRE

*Returning to her hometown, brokenhearted journalist
Adaline Harlow is supposed to write an exposé on
Colter Ward, Texas's Sexiest Bachelor, and that
assignment does not include falling for him! As the
attraction grows, will they break their no-love-allowed
rule for a second chance at happiness?*

Read on for a sneak peek at
Most Eligible Cowboy
by USA TODAY *bestselling author Stacey Kennedy.*

"You want your story. I want these women off my back…
Stay in town and agree to being my girlfriend until this
story dies down and I'll give you the exclusive you want."

"Her eyes widened. "You're serious?"

"Deadly serious," he confirmed. "I want my life back.
You need a promotion. This is a win-win for both of us."

She gave a cute wiggle on her stool. "I think you're
giving me far too much credit. Why would women care if
I'm your girlfriend?"

"I don't think you're giving yourself enough credit."
He stared at her parted lips, shining eyes, her slowly

building smile, and closed the distance between them, waiting for her to back away. When she didn't and even leaned in closer, he said, "Trust me, they'd care." He captured her mouth, cupping her warm face, telling himself the whole damn time this was a terrible idea.

Don't miss what happens next in...
Most Eligible Cowboy
by USA TODAY *bestselling author Stacey Kennedy.*

Available November 2022 wherever
Harlequin Desire books and ebooks are sold.

Harlequin.com

Love Harlequin romance?

DISCOVER.

Be the first to find out about promotions,
news and exclusive content!

Facebook.com/HarlequinBooks

Twitter.com/HarlequinBooks

Instagram.com/HarlequinBooks

Pinterest.com/HarlequinBooks

YouTube.com/HarlequinBooks

ReaderService.com

EXPLORE.

Sign up for the Harlequin e-newsletter and
download a free book from any series at
TryHarlequin.com

CONNECT.

Join our Harlequin community to
share your thoughts and connect
with other romance readers!
Facebook.com/groups/HarlequinConnection

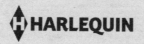

HARLEQUIN

Heartfelt or thrilling, passionate or uplifting—Harlequin is more than just happily-ever-after.

With twelve different series to choose from and new books available every month, you are sure to find stories that will move you, uplift you, inspire and delight you.

SIGN UP FOR THE HARLEQUIN NEWSLETTER

Be the first to hear about great new reads and exciting offers!

Harlequin.com/newsletters

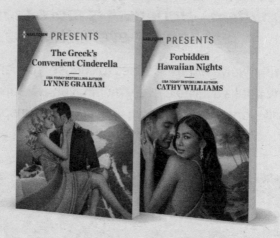